"Send them in."

Julie's assistant allowed the man and dog to enter.
Julie glanced up to greet her client and—

Whoa!

She leaned back in surprise. He was so…so
handsome. Not classically so, but in a kind of way
that exuded power and confidence. A deep chest
and well-shaped head. Definitely a male in his
prime. Something in his eyes tugged at her heart.
Made her—

"Miss Jones?"

The deep voice was rough and caused a warning
tingle at her nape. Reluctantly Julie tore her gaze
from the mastiff's to look at the man and—

Whoa!

Her eyes widened. The man standing just inside
her door didn't look like a man who would back
down for anyone. Like his dog's, the man's eyes
were also brown, also intelligent. But these dark
eyes held a critical, assessing glint as he eyed her
from the doorway, making her stiffen.

Yes, she was in trouble!

Dear Reader,

No month better suits Silhouette Romance than February. For it celebrates that breathless feeling of first love, the priceless experiences and memories that come with a longtime love and the many hopes and dreams that give a couple's life together so much meaning. At Silhouette Romance, our writers try to capture all these feelings in their timeless tales…and this month's lineup is no exception.

Our PERPETUALLY YOURS promotion continues this month with a charming tale from Sandra Paul. In *Domesticating Luc* (#1802) a dog trainer gets more than she bargained for when she takes on an unruly puppy and his very obstinate and irresistible owner. Beloved author Judy Christenberry returns to the lineup with *Honeymoon Hunt* (#1803)—a madcap adventure in which two opposites pair up to find their parents who have eloped, but instead wind up on a tight race to the finish line, er, altar! In *A Dash of Romance* (#1804) Elizabeth Harbison creates the perfect recipe for love when she pairs a self-made billionaire with a spirited waitress. Cathie Linz rounds out the offerings with *Lone Star Marine* (#1805). Part of her MEN OF HONOR series, this poignant romance features a wounded soldier who craves only the solitude to heal, and finds that his lively and beautiful neighbor just might be the key to the future he hadn't dreamed possible.

As always, be sure to return next month when Alice Sharpe concludes our PERPETUALLY YOURS promotion.

Happy reading.

Ann Leslie Tuttle
Associate Senior Editor

Please address questions and book requests to:
Silhouette Reader Service
U.S.: 3010 Walden Ave., P.O. Box 1325, Buffalo, NY 14269
Canadian: P.O. Box 609, Fort Erie, Ont. L2A 5X3

Domesticating Luc

SANDRA PAUL

PerPetually
Yours

SILHOUETTE *Romance*®
Published by Silhouette Books
America's Publisher of Contemporary Romance

This book is dedicated to Duke, Sissy, Sammy, Buddy, Cherokee, Fantasy, Popeye, Shorty, Ruby, and— last but not least—our gentle giant Thor.

 SILHOUETTE BOOKS

ISBN 0-373-19802-7

DOMESTICATING LUC

Visit Silhouette Books at www.eHarlequin.com

Printed in U.S.A.

Books by Sandra Paul

Silhouette Romance

Last Chance for Marriage #883
The Reluctant Hero #1016
His Accidental Angel #1087
The Makeover Takeover #1559
Caught by Surprise #1614
Domesticating Luc #1802

SANDRA PAUL

married her high school sweetheart and they live in Southern California. They have three children, three cats and one overgrown "puppy."

Sandra has a degree in journalism, but prefers to write from the heart. When she isn't busy working as a housekeeper, gardener, animal trainer, short-order cook, accountant, caregiver, interior designer, nutritional researcher, chauffeur, hotline love adviser, handywoman, landscape architect, business consultant, or serving as the primary volunteer for the Rocking Horse Rescue, she loves to create stories that end in happily ever after.

Sandra and her "suite-est" critiquing buddies can be reached at www.RomanceNovelistsSuite.com.

Dear Reader,

While working on a small weekly newspaper, I once had to interview a dog.

"C'mon," I moaned, when given the assignment. "Dogs can't talk."

"According to her owner, Ginger can," my editor replied unsympathetically. "Give me five hundred words."

Ginger, I soon discovered, was a small, spaniel-beagle-whatever mix. According to her owner, Jo, "She was the only one at the pound who wasn't barking and begging, 'Take me! Take me!' She just sat there looking at me with her big, sad eyes." Jo petted the little dog sitting beside her, adding, "They say it's a sign of intelligence to know when not to speak."

I looked at Ginger. She looked at me. And she didn't speak a word. Obviously, a *very* intelligent animal. Which didn't bode well for my five hundred words.

"So what does she say?" I demanded.

"Only the most important thing." Jo cradled Ginger's hairy face in her hands. The little dog met her eyes intently as Jo crooned, "I love you, Ginger. I *love* you!"

"Oo—oo—oooo!" Ginger crooned back.

Okay, so her accent was a little ruff. That really doesn't matter when you listen with your heart. And with her adoring eyes, wiggling body and furiously wagging tail, Ginger definitely managed to get her message across.

Just like dogs everywhere.

Thank you so much for picking up Puppy's story. I sincerely hope you enjoy it.

Sandra Paul

Pawlogue

The Man was leaving.

The signs were obvious—the jingle of his keys, the scent of the leather briefcase he always took with him, the man-leash he'd draped around his neck.

Even from outside, watching through the screen door leading to the backyard patio, I could tell he was impatient to get away. But the bitch who'd arrived a few minutes earlier appeared to be surprised. In the month that I'd lived at The Man's house, other women had visited him, but I'd never seen this one before. Skinny as an alley cat, her eyes were ringed with black and she had multicolored fur on her head—light in the front and dark in the back.

"You're going into work? On a Saturday?" she asked as he paused in front of the hall mirror to knot his leash around his throat.

"Yeah."

"But I thought we'd spend the day together," she purred, brushing against his arm.

Something in her manner reminded me of a Siamese cat I used to know. Sinuous and sly, she circled The Man, trying to get his attention. "Wouldn't it be fun to go swimming?" she coaxed, moving close to him again.

"Not today," The Man replied as he finished adjusting his leash. I wasn't fond of cats and apparently, The Man wasn't either. Because when she rubbed against his arm again, he stepped away. "I have too much work to get through." He picked up his briefcase. "You should have called before you came over."

"I wanted to surprise you."

"You certainly accomplished that. What's it been? Eight months? Ten?"

Her eyes narrowed. "Four months."

"That long, huh? Time sure flies, doesn't it?"

She ignored the comment to plead, "Can't you stay?"

"Sorry, no." But he didn't sound sorry. Or even very interested as he added, "But you're welcome to use the pool before you go."

She must have heard the indifference in his voice, because her mouth grew tight. She glanced away from him to hide her reaction and caught sight of me. "Oh! You got a dog!" she exclaimed.

"Not really. He was my aunt's." The Man glanced impatiently at his watch. "Leila—"

"What an interesting animal! He's so huge!" she interrupted, sauntering in my direction. She peered at me. Her scent crept beneath the door. She smelled like crushed flowers, mixed indiscriminately together in a tangled mass.

"Nice doggy," she said, in a gushy, high voice that made the hair rise along my back. "What a cute little doggy-oggy you are." She pursed her mouth in a kissy-face.

I prudently moved back a few feet.

She glanced over her shoulder at The Man. "I just love dogs!" she declared.

Her tone annoyed me. When she looked at me again, I deliberately looked away.

"And apparently, they love you, too," The Man said sardonically. His voice hardened with impatience—a tone I was very familiar with. "Now do you want to use the pool or not?"

"All alone?"

"That's right."

"But what about the dog?"

"He doesn't like to swim."

The bitch smiled, but I could tell she wasn't amused. "I meant, will he bother me?"

"No. He just lies around all day. Besides, I thought you *loved* dogs."

They stared at each other, her expression entreating, his unbending. "I don't think I will go swimming today," she finally said, her voice stiff.

"Suit yourself." The Man opened the door, then paused a moment on the threshold. Sparing me a glance, he added, "But if you do stay, make sure you lock the French doors behind you, and don't leave the backyard gate open. He'll run away."

And without further comment, he left.

The bitch just stood there for a couple of seconds, staring at the closed door. Pity welled up inside me. I knew how painful it could be to be left behind.

Then, "Hateful man!" she spat viciously. "He hasn't changed a bit." She looked round and, catching my gaze, hissed, "Serve him right if I did let you out, you ugly monster."

The thought seemed to raise her spirits. She strode

over to the back door and undid the latch. She slid the glass open and stepped outside, circling around me to head toward the wrought iron gate beyond the pool and guesthouse.

When she'd gone about five yards, I stood up. She glanced over her shoulder. Her eyes widened as I started following her. She quickened her pace. So did I. She broke into a slow jog. So did I. She ran faster and— well, you get the idea.

By the time she reached the gate, sweat gleamed on her pale face. She threw herself against the wrought iron and looked at me, her eyes wild. "Good dog," she said, her voice shrill. "Good dog."

I sat down and barked in agreement with her assessment.

She cringed. Without taking her gaze off me, she undid the latch. She pushed the gate open. "There you go." She made a shooing gesture with her long clawed hands. "Scat. Go on. Run away."

Who did she think she was, giving me orders? I felt no need to obey her. Besides, no matter how much I wanted to, I couldn't leave. Not yet.

I yawned, then stood up.

She backed away a step. "Good lord, you have big teeth," she said, her own teeth chattering slightly. "Don't you dare bite me," she added in a warning tone, "I swear, I'll sue the pants off him if you do."

I wasn't planning on biting her; I'd been raised to be polite. But I didn't like her. I wanted her gone. I growled, long and low, to encourage her to be on her way.

She got the message. She swallowed and slunk through the gate, then broke into a sprint.

I watched as she raced to her car, resisting the urge to give chase. She certainly didn't run like a cat. I could have caught her in two major leaps. But I didn't have time to fool around.

Before the roar of her mechanical beast had faded into the distance, I turned and headed back to the glass door. Just as I'd suspected, she'd left it ajar. I nudged it open further with my muzzle until my head and shoulders could squeeze through.

I entered the house.

I'd been inside before, three years ago when I'd been just a pup. The scents, the sounds, wafting in the air nudged my memory of that brief visit. The tart scent of lemon and beeswax emanating from the dark glossy furniture. The brisk, tight tick of a tall clock standing in the hallway. Nothing appeared changed. Surely what I sought was still here.

Eager to find out, my pace quickened. My nails clicked on the cold marble tiles in the kitchen, then on the shiny hardwood floors as I made my way down the hall to find the room I'd visited long ago. A familiar scent tickled my nostrils, and I lifted my head higher to sniff the air. The scent grew stronger the nearer I drew to the open doors before me, and with three more loping strides, I entered a large room.

I hesitated a moment on the threshold, my paws sinking into a carpet as soft as a bed of moss. Was this the room we'd sat in? It smelled the same. The heavy scent of the leather couch squatting before the fireplace filled the air—a smell so rich, so enticing that drool gathered in my jowls.

Still, I wasn't quite sure. So I explored the room thoroughly—sniffing carefully around the sleek, cold hearth, tracking my way slowly across the carpet nearby. Instinct guided me as I pushed my muzzle deep into the thick pile, snuffling intently until—

Aha! This *was* the right room! Deep in the fibers, I caught the faint, barely discernible trace of the small stain I'd left there as a youngster. I circled the area, sniffing intently. The urge to cover the spot again was strong…but I was no longer a pup. I knew now I didn't belong here.

This was The Man's territory, not mine.

So, I turned away from the distraction and headed toward the leather couch. I'd do what I had to do, and then be on my way. With a small "woof" of determination, I got to work.

And two hours later—fourteen hours in dog time— I found what I'd been searching for.

Chapter One

Selecting a puppy:

Picking the perfect puppy isn't easy. Size, weight and breed all need to be considered. But the most important factor is the temperament of your animal.

To evaluate the social tendencies of your choice, watch how he interacts with others. Does he approach in a stiff-legged manner? Is his tail tucked beneath his bottom? Is he confident in his stance? Is he excitable or calm? Does he bark incessantly or whimper? Does he bite? Or cower?

You don't want a timid animal. But you most certainly don't want one that is aggressive.
Evaluating That Puppy in the Window, Dr. Louis Kaku

"**I** give up."

"Hmm?" Julie Jones, owner of the Puppy Love Dog Training Institute, glanced up from the ledger she'd been comparing to the accounts on her computer. Brushing a strand of dark hair out of her eyes, she focused on the woman planted in front of her desk. "What did you say, Georgia?"

"I said I give up," the gray-haired trainer repeated, folding her muscular arms across her chest. "Our newest client is completely untrainable. He snarls, he growls. He refuses to obey the simplest command without balking. He's disrupting the whole class. There's no way he's going to pass basic training."

"Oh, dear." Julie leaned back in her chair, biting her lower lip. She was so proud of the stellar record of the institute, which was earning a reputation among dog owners in the west Los Angeles area as the best place to take problem pooches. Never once in the two years since she'd bought the facility had they had a failure. "He's that bad, huh?"

"Yes!" declared Georgia, with an emphatic nod of her head. "Completely hopeless—a real son of a bitch." She considered the matter, then added, "And his dog isn't much better."

"Aggressive?"

"Not the dog. Just the man. A bit intimidating. He's not very friendly to the other owners. Tends to snap at them." Her glasses slid down her pug nose. She pushed them back up. "He's also expecting instant results, and that's not going to happen. The dog simply isn't responding."

Julie sighed and set down her pen. "All right. Send them in. I'll see if I can figure out what the problem is."

While Georgia went to fetch the pair, Julie shut down

her computer, then hunted for their file among the stacks on her desk. She started with the largest pile—clients who owed money—but after diligently digging found it in the thinnest heap—prepaid accounts.

She opened up the manilla folder. Paper-clipped to the top was a check signed in a dark slashing hand by a Lucien Tagliano. Glancing at the amount, the tension in her shoulders eased a bit. He'd paid for a full three months in advance. Not only would the money help pay the bills, it also showed Tagliano was committed to training his dog.

Feeling more hopeful, she lifted the check to read the information sheet below it. Tagliano was listed as the animal's owner on the form, which also gave his occupation—business owner—and his home address in an exclusive part of the city.

But the information on his pet was scanty. Julie was frowning over the omissions when a brief tap on the open door heralded Georgia's return. The trainer poked her head around the jamb. "They're here."

Julie nodded. "Send them in."

Georgia opened the door wider to allow the man and dog to enter. Julie glanced up to greet her client and—

Whoa!

She leaned back in surprise. He was so...so *handsome*. Not classically so, but in a tough, rugged kind of way that exuded power and confidence. Wide, muscular shoulders. A deep chest and well-shaped head. Surely Italian, she thought, as he paced almost arrogantly into the room. Definitely a male in his prime. His brow and jaw were wide, his rough-hewn features so clearly defined he would have appeared almost brutal if it weren't for his eyes. Dark brown. Intelligent. Something in them tugged at her heart. Made her—

"Miss Jones?"

The deep voice was rough, like a growl, and caused a warning tingle at her nape. Reluctantly, Julie tore her gaze from the mastiff's to look at the man and—

Whoa!

Her eyes widened. The man standing just inside her door certainly didn't look like a businessman. His long-sleeved white dress shirt and dark slacks might be traditional business attire, but, like a pink satin bow on a timber wolf, did nothing to disguise the true nature of the beast. Well over six feet tall, his broad shoulders and muscular arms were clearly defined beneath his shirt, and the leather belt on the slacks encircled a lean waist and hips. His brow was wide, his cheekbones high and prominent, his square jaw shadowed. His thick, dark brown hair was cropped short in a severe style that did nothing to soften his chiseled features. His masculine nose was slightly battered, as if he'd broken it.

Probably in a fight, Julie thought, meeting his gaze. He looked like a man who wouldn't back down from anyone. Like his dog's, the man's eyes were also brown, also intelligent. But these dark eyes held a critical, assessing glint that made her stiffen as he eyed her from the doorway.

"Yes, I'm Miss Jones," she acknowledged, as he strode toward her with the easy, powerful grace of a natural-born aggressor.

He held out his big, tanned hand. "Lucien Tagliano."

"Nice to meet you, Mr. Tagliano." She put her hand in his.

His long tanned fingers closed around hers, tightening just enough to reveal the controlled strength of his grasp. "Luc," he commanded.

"Julie," she replied and pulled away to gesture at the chair in front of her desk. "Please. Have a seat. I just want to write down a few observations before we begin."

His dark eyes narrowed, and his lips tightened. Julie waited, expecting him to argue, but he didn't. After a moment, he nodded and sat in the chair she had indicated.

Julie frowned at him thoughtfully. He should have appeared relaxed with his long legs stretched out and his hands tucked into the front pockets of his slacks, but a sense of coiled energy still emanated from his big frame, and his intense, assessing gaze continued to study her in a way that made her feel oddly wary. Despite the temptation to keep a cautious eye on him, she forced herself to look away, to concentrate on the dog sitting so quietly nearby.

Definitely a magnificent animal, she thought again, with his beautiful eyes, cropped ears and short, gleaming brown coat. To the uninitiated, the dog might appear to be a half-breed. Tougher looking than an English mastiff. More reminiscent of a cross between a bull dog and a rottweiller—a very big rottweiller. He had to weigh one hundred forty pounds at the least, and was superbly muscled with the large head, broad shoulders and slim haunches prized in his breed.

But something about the dog troubled her. Julie absently tapped her pen against the edge of her desk as she tried to figure out what the problem could be. Maybe it was the way he sat—with quiet dignity but as far away from his owner as the leash would allow. Not as if the animal were afraid—there were no indications of cowering or mistrust—but rather as if he were…indifferent. She jotted the word down. And although he'd

glanced around the room, looked at her, when he'd first
entered, there were none of the signs of eager interest
she would have expected of an animal entering un-
known territory. Instead, the mastiff simply sat there,
and, even as she watched, he lay down, placing his big
head on his paws.

She added *Appears surprisingly passive* to her notes,
along with observations about his weight, demeanor
and physical condition. Then she started filling in the
spaces Tagliano had left blank on the form, becoming
increasingly absorbed as she wrote.

And while Julie studied the dog, Luc Tagliano studied her.

At first, he thought her remark about taking notes
was simply a ploy—a way to impress him. After all, the
dog was just lying there. What was there to take notes
on? But after watching the woman for about a minute
or so, Luc realized she was truly engrossed in studying
the animal—and completely oblivious to him.

That surprised him; *she* surprised him.

If he'd thought about it—which he hadn't—he
would have expected the owner of this facility to resem-
ble the stern-faced instructor who'd led him to this office. But the only resemblance between the two women
that he could see were the bright blue shirts both wore
with the Puppy Love Institute logo discreetly stamped
above their right breasts.

In fact, Julie Jones didn't match his inner vision of
a dog trainer in the least. To begin with, she looked too
young to own this place. Twenty-five—twenty-eight
max. And everything about the woman appeared…soft.
Soft, wide mouth. Soft brown hair tumbling gently to
her shoulders. Soft, slender curves under her blue
blouse and dark pants. Soft, slender hands—surpris-

ingly bare of rings. Even her gray eyes looked soft.
When she was looking at the dog, anyway.

When she'd looked at *him,* it was a different matter.

Then her eyes turned cool, guarded, only warming
again when she looked at the mastiff. Which she'd done
unceasingly now for the past five minutes. Still totally
ignoring Luc.

Which was fine—great. Luc shifted in his chair.
Didn't bother him at all. Just not the usual female reaction to his presence, by any means. Still, all that mattered to him was getting the damn dog straightened out
as quickly as possible. He'd chosen the Puppy Love Institute on the recommendation of one of the general
contractors he often worked with and had been pleased
with the appearance of the place when he'd first arrived.
The main building appeared to be well-maintained, the
expansive lawns of the training grounds surrounding it
neatly trimmed. A wide track with an obstacle course
nearby was part of the setup, and even came equipped
with huge overhead lights for night classes.

Yeah, he'd been satisfied with the overall look of the
place, but less so with the class to which he and the dog
had been assigned. And he'd been *much* less approving
of its instructor, the prototype of a female prison guard.
Good lord, the woman could make most dogs—not to
mention humans—cower with the frown on her face
alone.

Definitely unlike Julie Jones, who was still scribbling furiously, small white teeth absently gnawing on
her lower lip as she concentrated. Too bad he'd left his
cell phone in his truck. He could have made a couple
of calls while waiting.

He thought about retrieving it, then decided not to
bother. This shouldn't take long. Curbing his impa-

tience, he glanced around the office. A dog calendar hung on a far wall next to a couple of puppy posters and several framed certificates. The most prominent informed those interested that Julie Ann Jones had received a bachelor's degree in psychology, with an emphasis on animal behavior. The rest appeared to be awards for various dog obedience competitions.

Luc glanced back at Julie. Light streamed through the large window behind her, haloing her brown hair and slender shoulders as she wrote and spilling across her desk. A small plastic bowl of cookies adorned one corner of the oak surface. A nameplate stating Miss Julie Jones—*so she wasn't married*—was centered at the front of the desk, and paperwork covered the rest.

Not very efficient, Luc thought, eyeing the mounds of folders. A well-chewed rubber bone adorned one pile, a bright yellow rubber duck another. A worn, dog-eared manual of an outdated accounting program sat next to her computer. The machine itself was downright antiquated. She obviously wasn't reinvesting her money in technology, but rather, it appeared, in the vast array of books she owned. He looked at the bookshelves flanking the window. Both of the cases were tightly packed from floor to ceiling.

He narrowed his eyes, scanning the titles. *When Lassie Won't Come Home. Controlling Canine Capers. Dealing with Doggy Disobedience.* Most appeared to be books on dog behavior. But a good number were also about individual breeds. Poodles. Terriers. Dachshunds. Rottweillers. Dobermans. German shepherds. Sporting dogs. Working dogs. Show dogs. The list was endless.

With a shake of his head, he looked at Julie again. A frown creased her smooth brow as she jotted something on the paper before her. He shifted again, but she still didn't look up. A phone rang somewhere down the hall and in the distance, he could hear the steel-haired trainer barking "Heel!" and "Sit!" at the class he'd been expelled from. He glanced at his Rolex and straightened in his chair. Okay, enough was enough. He wanted to get some work done this evening, not hang around here all night.

He opened his mouth, but before he could speak, Julie finally paused in her scribbling to glance his way. "Italian?" she asked

Okay, so maybe she wasn't quite as oblivious to him as she'd seemed. Luc nodded, settling back in his chair. "Yeah, my parents moved from Italy to New York in their early twenties. I moved out here when I was in my teens."

Julie stared at him a moment. "That's interesting," she said politely. "But I was talking about your dog."

Oh. The dog. Luc frowned at the mastiff, then shrugged. "I'm not sure. I inherited him from my aunt. She died a month ago."

"I'm sorry." For the first time, her gaze softened as she met his eyes. Hers were a darker gray than he'd first thought. Like soft smoke, with thick, sooty lashes. She looked at the dog again. "What's his name?"

"Primus Del Colosseo is on his papers. It means King of the Colosseum in Italian," he added in response to her questioning glance.

"You speak it?"

"Yeah. Since I was a kid."

"I see. King of the Colosseum," she repeated, tapping her pen thoughtfully against her notes. "Well, that makes sense."

"It does?"

"Of course. Don't you know what kind of dog this is?"

"A mastiff."

"Yes, but not just any mastiff." She rose from her chair and came around the desk. Her dark blue pants encased slim hips and long legs, Luc noted.

Resting her bottom against her desk, she looked down at the dog in admiration. "I've only seen them in pictures," she admitted, "but I'm almost positive this is a *Cane corso,* a very rare Italian breed of mastiff. It's believed the *Cane corso* stems directly from the giant Molossus, the giant war dog of ancient Rome, which was not only used in battle against the enemy, but also spent time with lions and gladiators in the great amphitheaters."

Wryly, Luc shook his head. "A war dog, huh? Trust Great-Aunt Sophia to choose a completely inappropriate dog for a pet just because it's Italian."

"In my opinion, your great-aunt made a good choice when she selected this breed," Julie said firmly. "These dogs are known for their agility and speed—they were used for generations in Italy to catch cattle as well as to guard herds and flocks. It's true they are loners by nature, and their less desirable characteristics can include stubbornness and a desire to control those around them. But if socialized correctly, they can be a very discriminating and effective protector of the home."

"That's good to know."

"Nor do they drool like other mastiffs."

"Even better," Luc said, looking at the mastiff's wide mouth.

Julie nodded, her gaze warm as she also looked at the dog. The warmth faded as she glanced back up at Luc. "I understand from Ms. Irenmadden that you're a—having a problem in our basic training class."

"The only problem I'm having is that the class is a complete waste of time," Luc corrected her grimly. "As I tried to explain to Miss Iron Maiden—"

"Ms. Irenmadden."

"—this dog doesn't need basic training. He already had all that when he was with my aunt. He needs more specific help."

"I see," Julie said noncommittally. Putting down her pen, she leaned toward the dog and snapped her fingers lightly to catch his attention.

The big head lifted and he looked at her inquiringly.

"Here, Primus," she called softly. "Here, boy."

Her voice was warm, sweet. Soothing and enticing, Luc admitted. But the dog didn't even move.

Julie glanced Luc's way, her slim eyebrows arched in curiosity. "He's had basic training, but he doesn't respond to his name?"

Luc shifted in his chair, then settled again. "My aunt never called him by name. She simply called him—" He hesitated, then stated through clenched teeth, "Puppy."

The dog's ears pricked forward.

"Puppy," Julie repeated, her smoky eyes lighting up. The dog looked at her. "That's so—"

"Ridiculous."

"I was going to say sweet." She walked back around her desk and sat down, picking up her pen. "But the most important thing is, he responds to it. And if you want to bond with this dog—"

"I don't."

She lifted her head. "I beg your pardon?"

"I don't want to bond with the animal. All I want to do is find him a good home. That's what I promised my great-aunt before she died, so that's what I'll do. But no way am I keeping him myself."

Her soft mouth pressed into a firm line. "I see." She tapped her pen on the papers before her. "So why haven't you placed him somewhere?"

"I thought I had," Luc said grimly. "Several times. And each time he's been returned to me in less than a day. At the first place, he took down a gate along with a section—a very long section—of fence to escape. At another, he wouldn't stop howling—kept it up for eight straight hours. At the last place, he dug a hole so deep to get out under a wall I'm surprised the blocks didn't collapse on him. And then there's his chewing."

"Most dogs chew—"

"I'm not talking slippers here," Luc interrupted. "I'm talking about my couch—a Pablo Hvostal original I bought just three years ago for seven thousand dollars."

"Oh, dear." Julie bit her lip, looking at the dog again.

"Believe me, *oh, dear* doesn't begin to cover it. Worst of all, his bad behavior is escalating. He's begun growling if anyone goes near the dog crate where he sleeps, and one of my…guests recently claimed that he menaced her, chased her right out of my yard."

Julie looked concerned. "He bit her?"

"No, but she said he tried to. I'm not sure I believe her, however," Luc admitted. "I suspect if this animal tried to bite, he probably wouldn't miss with a mouth that size. Still, I can't take the chance he's turning vicious. Which is why I thought I'd better get some professional help with him."

Julie nodded in agreement, her considering gaze still fixed on the mastiff. She watched him for a second, then looked back at Luc. Her expression turned earnest. "I can understand your frustration. That's a completely normal reaction under the circumstances."

"Thank you," he said dryly.

"But you need to understand that all these undesirable behaviors are correctable."

Luc nodded abruptly. "Good. Because that's exactly why I brought him here. So you can correct them."

"But I'm not the one Puppy needs. *You* are." Seeing his eyes narrow, she spread her hands in an encompassing gesture, adding, "In a dog's mind, there is no problem behavior. Everything he does, he does for a reason. And what you've described—the barking, the chewing, the running away—are all indications of stress. Our classes will help divert Puppy and keep him occupied, but what he obviously craves most is companionship. It sounds as if he's been 'acting out' in a bid for your attention."

Luc straightened in his chair. "Are you trying to tell me this dog is misbehaving because he wants to get closer to me?"

"I'm almost positive of it," Julie maintained. "Although all dogs are individuals, just like humans, and every situation is unique. But in any event, it's obvious that Puppy is unhappy about something. He needs retraining, and he needs socialization. But most of all, he needs affection. *Your* affection…."

Luc listened without comment as she rambled on about "a dog's secret desire to please his master" and the "possible damage to Puppy's delicate emotional state" if nothing was done. Then, as she concluded her encouraging little speech about "love being the best motivator to good animal behavior," Luc stood up to leave.

Julie Jones might be a sexy little thing. She might even appear to be fairly intelligent.

But she was obviously insane.

Controlling his temper with an effort, he said, "Look,

maybe you mean well. Maybe you even believe what you're saying, and are not just spouting some kind of sappy sales pitch to get more money out of me."

Her shoulders stiffened. "I assure you—"

"You don't need to assure me of anything," Luc interrupted, "because I can tell you this. That dog—" he pointed at Puppy, who cocked his head inquiringly at the gesture "—doesn't need love. He needs discipline. For God's sake, I brought him here to be *trained*, not psychoanalyzed."

Puppy rose to his feet, leashing trailing on the floor, as Luc continued, "He's a *dog*, damn it. He doesn't have an emotional state. All he cares about is eating, sleeping and destroying everything in sight. He's simply a stubborn, recalcitrant, big hairy animal that hasn't shown a scrap of interest, much less affection, for anyone in all the time I've had—"

He broke off. Puppy had walked over to Julie and was now standing close, staring at her intently.

Very intently.

Remembering Leila's claim about the animal's aggression, Luc tensed, preparing to grab the leash.

Then Puppy lowered his massive head. Stepping closer, the dog nudged Julie's arm gently with his muzzle, clearly inviting a pet.

Julie obliged, then glanced at Luc and raised her eyebrows inquiringly. "You were saying?" she asked sweetly.

Chapter Two

The dog's pedigree:

Scientists believe the dog's lineage began over 37 million years ago in predators that chased down prey. Ten million more years passed before the genus *Canis* emerged, from which gradually developed *Canis lupus,* or the wolf.

The wolf is the ancestor of all present-day dogs. At the molecular level, the DNA makeup of wolves and dogs is almost identical. Although domestication is the balm applied to tame the savage beast, deep beneath their fur every dog—from the tiniest Chihuahua to the most massive mastiff—believes he is a wolf.

Barking Up the Dog's Family Tree, Allen Mavis, Ph.D.

Luc's dropped jaw snapped shut. He felt like a fool, but not such a complete fool that he couldn't recognize a golden opportunity when he saw one. "You take him."

Her eyes widened. "What?"

"*You* take him. Look, the dog appears to actually *like* you—"

"Well, he seems—"

"And you like him, right?"

"Of course, but—"

"So you can have him. He's all yours, free of charge. It's the perfect answer all around."

Julie drew a deep breath. "Perfect for you, maybe," she said dryly. "Hardly perfect for me, or even Puppy. I honestly believe this dog will respond better to you."

Luc shook his head. Respond better to him? She *was* crazy. Anyone with an ounce of sense could see she was the one Puppy belonged with. She cared about animals. He knew it—hell, the dog knew it. She'd already started petting the mastiff again—scratching behind his ears, beneath his chin, along his thick neck. And, judging by the big, goofy grin on the animal's face, the dog was loving it.

Maybe a little pressure would do the trick. "I'd hate to ask for my money back," Luc said softly.

Her hand stilled, and her head snapped up. Puppy lifted his head, as well, disturbed that the petting had halted. Julie gave the dog a regretful glance, then folded her hands on her desk. She looked over at Luc, steadily meeting his gaze. "And I'd hate to return your money," she said. "But if a refund is what you want—"

"No, that's not what I want, damn it," Luc conceded, exhaling in exasperation. Reaching for his chair, he yanked it closer and sat back down. "What I want is help getting this dog in shape so I can fulfill my promise to my aunt. Believe me, even perfectly behaved, this isn't the type of dog that appeals to that many people."

Julie's tense expression eased a fraction. "I know. But I can't take him, even if I thought he'd do better with me. I have no place to keep him. My present apartment is being converted into condos and I'll be living in a motel for the next couple of months, starting Saturday."

"Take him after that."

"After that, I'll be living in my *new* apartment, which unfortunately, doesn't allow dogs."

"So find another one."

Julie stared at him. "Easy for you to say. Do you know how expensive rentals are in this city? I'm lucky I found the one that I did."

"You could keep him here."

She looked horrified. "I just told you he needs to spend time with people. There's no way I'd leave him here alone every night."

Luc opened his mouth to continue the argument, but Julie forestalled him. "No, I'm sorry, but Puppy is your responsibility, not mine," she said firmly. "You admit that it's been impossible to place him with the behavior problems he's exhibiting, so if you want him to have a good home—"

"I told you, I promised my aunt I'd find him one."

"Then *work* with him for a while! I'm convinced that he'll respond very rapidly to you—once you put some effort into the relationship," she added pointedly.

Luc ignored her gibe about making an effort, intent on deciding how best to handle the situation. Because he wasn't about to abandon what was obviously the perfect solution all around. *He* couldn't keep the animal. Even if he wanted to—which he didn't—he'd be traveling to Costa Rica in about a month, and then probably on to Europe after that, to check on a couple projects he had going there. He wasn't home enough to own a fish, much less a dog.

Besides, no matter what she said, he was positive Julie Jones was the one who should own the mastiff. She was the kind of woman he suspected his aunt would have liked. Independent. Kind. Definitely an animal lover. If he could get her to take the dog, his obligation to Aunt Sophia would be more than fulfilled.

He studied the determination in Julie's expression— her narrowed eyes, the stubborn tilt of her cute chin. The problem, he decided, was that they'd gotten off to a rocky start here. Not only had he put her back up with his dismissal of her initial diagnosis of the mastiff, he hadn't improved matters by threatening to take back his money.

He suspected professional pride as much as practical considerations was now keeping her from backing down and accepting the animal. Judging by her squared shoulders, Julie was obviously braced to resist Luc at this point, to counter whatever he said. Pushing now would simply strengthen her resolve.

Yeah, he'd definitely screwed up. He'd neglected to follow the basic rule of negotiation that had gotten him ahead in the business world for the last ten years: find out what the opponent needs and offer it.

With a few minor conditions, of course.

His gaze roamed over Julie's stubborn face again. Time to change tactics.

He smiled.

She blinked in surprise. Then she leaned back and folded her arms across her chest, keeping her wary gaze fixed on Luc.

"You're completely right," he said, smoothly. "The animal—er, Puppy—is my responsibility, of course, not yours. But maybe there's a compromise here that could benefit us both."

She started to shake her head, so he continued rapidly, "You need a place to stay for the next couple of weeks and Puppy and I need some one-on-one tutoring. It just so happens there's an empty guesthouse on my property. It's not very large, but it's comfortably furnished, and you can use the pool, too, if you like. How 'bout you stay there for a few weeks—free of charge—in return for some professional advice?"

Her expression didn't just cool; it froze. "I couldn't possibly impose on you and your wife that way."

"I'm not married."

That didn't appear to reassure her. Her full lips flattened into a thin line. "I couldn't impose on *you*, then."

Luc bit back an impatient retort. Taking a deep breath, he said, "You wouldn't be imposing. The guesthouse is completely separate from the main building. We wouldn't have to see each other at all, except when dealing with Puppy."

"Even so, I know nothing about you."

"So what do you want to know? I'm thirty-four. I own my own business. Here—" he reached into his back pocket and pulled out his wallet, tossing it onto her desk "—check my license, my credit cards. I'll even provide references if you want. Business associates, neighbors. The parish priest, if that'll clinch the deal." Mentally, he crossed his fingers on the last offer. The only time he'd been to church in the past ten years was for his aunt's funeral.

She still looked unconvinced, so he added in his most persuasive tones, "C'mon, Julie. It would be a trade-off, beneficial to us both." He spread out his hands, trying to appear as innocent and nonthreatening as possible. "What could be better? You'll get a place to stay. I'll get some on-the-spot advice on how to handle the dog."

Julie picked up her pen again, idly fingering it as she studied the man across from her. He put his hands in his pockets and leaned back in his chair, stretching out his long legs again in that casual, relaxed pose that should have been disarming. Still, Julie wasn't fooled. His East Coast Italian accent had thickened as he argued, augmenting his Big-Apple-in-your-face attitude.

Yes, his expression might be bland, his hard features unrevealing, but she knew exactly what was going on behind those heavy-lidded brown eyes.

Luc Tagliano thought she was a sucker.

He thought he had her all figured out. That he could get her to train Puppy, and convince her to keep the mastiff in the end. When his not-so-veiled threat to take back his money hadn't worked, he'd devised this scheme. She suspected that bulldog stubborn didn't even begin to describe the man when it came to getting his way.

She opened her mouth to tell him no—then paused when, from the corner of her eye, she caught sight of Puppy's forlorn expression. As a child, her dog Sissy had been her one constant companion as her family moved from one military base to another. After Sissy had died, her mother had allowed her to foster puppies to be trained as guide dogs and, while working at the institute, she'd come in contact with hundreds of dogs. But never had she felt such an instant connection with an animal as she had with the huge mastiff sitting with such forlorn dignity beside her.

The dog's apathy worried her. And something in his brown eyes tugged at her heart. She knew he wasn't her responsibility…but if she didn't help poor Puppy, who would?

All Luc Tagliano cared about was getting the dog off his hands.

She glanced back at Luc. He smiled at her again, revealing strong white teeth, all perfectly straight except for his incisors. Both jutted forward slightly, giving even his most innocent appearing smile—and oh, was he trying hard to appear innocent!—a slightly wolfish cast.

She tapped her pen absently on the desk as she continued to eye him. To give the devil his due, although he was more than assertive, Luc Tagliano also appeared to be a man of his word. Not many people—especially not many non-animal lovers—would go to so much trouble for a dog they clearly didn't want just to keep their word to a deceased relative. And it was that quality—as well as his stubbornness—that convinced her more than ever that Luc was the perfect owner for Puppy.

Because he was right about one thing: Puppy wasn't the type of dog people took to on sight. A big dog like this—a tough breed like the *Cane corso*—took very special handling.

Animals always responded best to strong-willed people. And Luc Tagliano obviously had the determined, masterful temperament, as well as the material resources, to take on such a large dog. No question there. But Julie also suspected that not only would this man be good for Puppy, Puppy would be good for this man. Playing with the dog might help him release some of that coiled tension so apparent in his big frame.

So, maybe two could play *this* game. Luc wanted her to bond with Puppy; she wanted Luc to. So she'd go along with his scheme and move into his guesthouse. Not only would she save a bit on rent, but even more importantly, she'd be on hand to oversee the situation. To nudge the two together, so they could learn to get along.

"You agree that you'll be Puppy's primary care-taker?" she asked.

Luc smiled again, white teeth flashing in his bronzed face. "Of course."

"And you'll continue with his basic training class?"

Luc's smile faded a bit. "I told you my aunt took him to classes—"

"He needs a refresher course."

"But you'll be there at the house to supervise one-on-one training."

"He still needs socialization with other dogs."

"The classes start too early for me to get here twice a week."

"Georgia has a Saturday class. You could switch to that one."

No longer smiling, Luc stared at her, obviously searching mentally for a loophole he could squeeze through. When he couldn't come up with one, he finally conceded, "All right, then. I'll switch to the Saturday class."

"Good." *One battle won.* "And you'll also need to spend time with him each day. On a regular schedule."

Luc's satisfied expression had given way to suspicion. "How much time?"

"At least two hours in the evenings."

He straightened in his chair. "Two hours? I just told you. I work late most nights and I travel—"

"You'll have to pass on that for a while. Puppy needs the time with you."

Luc looked at Puppy. Puppy returned his regard impassively. Luc thought about the business projects he had lined up and crossed his arms over his broad chest. "That's too much time out of my schedule."

Julie set down her pen. She began to straighten the papers on her desk, saying in a dismissive tone, "I understand completely. We'll just forget this whole idea and—"

"I'll do it for a month."

Julie frowned. A month wasn't very long. "I'm not sure…"

Luc gritted his teeth. He thought about his upcoming trip to Costa Rica to determine whether to build a resort there, the work he'd have if the project went through—and how much scrambling he'd have to do to rearrange things. He thought about his promise to his aunt. His jaw tightened.

"Six weeks," he finally growled. "I'll cut back for six weeks."

Julie considered the offer. Six weeks should be sufficient time for even a hard case like Luc to become attached to a sweet dog like Puppy, she decided. She held out her hand. "Then you have a deal."

Luc stood up to leave. Julie Jones drove a hard bargain, but he'd gotten what he wanted. She was a softie; no doubt about it. *She'll end up taking the dog in the end,* he thought. *She won't be able to help herself.*

He reached out his hand to meet hers, and once again, Julie briefly clasped his warm calloused palm. She met his wolfish smile with a serene expression, a warm glow of satisfaction in her heart. *Puppy is the perfect companion for a man like this,* she thought. *Luc'll keep the dog in the end; he won't be able to help himself.*

Luc released her hand. Picking up Puppy's leash, he headed for the door. Just before he stepped into the hall, however, he paused, looking back at Julie. "So I'll expect you this Friday night."

She shook her head. "My car will be in the shop Friday. Saturday will be better."

No way was he giving her a chance to back out at the last minute, Luc decided. "Where do you live?"

She told him, and he nodded abruptly. "I know the area. Don't worry about your car. I'll pick you up on Friday after work with my truck and help you move your stuff."

Her eyes widened in faint alarm. "There's no need—"

"You have someone else lined up to help you? Your family?"

"My family all lives out of state."

"A fiancé, then? A boyfriend? A friend?"

She stiffened defensively. "No, I planned to call a moving company—"

"No need. I'll do it—no problem," Luc said, cutting off her protests. "We'll get you settled in, and then we'll pick up your car the next day."

Without giving her time to argue further, he went out the door, Puppy at his heels.

For a long moment after they'd left, Julie remained in her chair, gripping the edges of her seat as if a strong wind might suddenly lift her out of it. Because that was exactly how she felt. As if a strong, determined wind had swept in and out of her office, whisking her around in a completely different direction.

She couldn't believe she'd agreed to live with that

man—a complete stranger, and a client to boot. But she had. For Puppy's sake.

Thinking about the dog, she released her grip on the chair and stood up, turning to stare out the window behind her to watch them leave. Luc and Puppy were striding across the parking lot toward a large, silver pickup, the kind with massive wheels that lifted it high off the ground. The big man and dog looked so right together, she thought again. Both rugged, both muscular, both so arrogantly male.

But not once did the man look down at the dog by his side. And not once did the dog look up at the man.

For the first time, a frisson of doubt shook her. She crossed her arms, hugging her waist as she continued to watch the pair. Had she made a mistake? Would she be able to get the two to bond?

They reached the truck. She half expected Luc to open the tailgate to let Puppy ride in the empty bed— a practice she heartily disapproved of—but to her relief he opened the passenger door for the animal instead. Both stood there a moment, neither moving as Luc looked down at the animal.

Then Luc suddenly bent and lifted the huge mastiff onto the seat.

Julie's mouth dropped open in surprise. Why had Luc lifted Puppy up like that? The truck was high, but the mastiff still should have been able to jump up onto the seat without any trouble at all. Was Puppy hurt somehow? Did he have a hip or back injury that she'd missed?

Concerned about the possibility, she continued watching until the truck pulled out of sight. Then, making a mental note to ask Luc about the incident when he and Puppy came to pick her up in a couple of days, she turned back to her desk. Sitting down, she started working on her accounts again, adding up numbers, penciling in figures. But beneath her preoccupation with the bills and her concern about Puppy, a faint alarm continued to hum along her nerves whenever she thought about seeing Luc again on Friday.

Because helping Puppy was one thing, but doing so on Luc Tagliano's territory was quite another.

Chapter Three

House training:

Is your home puppyproof? Is there anything there that can hurt your pet? To make sure there is nothing that can harm your animal, lead a dog's life for a while.

Become a puppy.

Get down on your hands and knees. Crawl under tables and behind couches. Sniff everything thoroughly. Roll around a bit. Bark at the house cat and caged birds to see how they react. Check the place out from your puppy's perspective.

Be as one with your pet.

The Zen of Puppy Training, Ray Angelino

Luc was alone when he arrived at Julie's two days later to help her move.

She answered her front door quickly in response to

his sharp knock, as if, Luc thought, she'd been watching for him. The possibility pleased him. He'd been looking forward to seeing her again, too.

He tipped the brim of his baseball cap up a bit and let his gaze, shielded behind mirrored sunglasses, run quickly over her. The slight swell of her breasts pressed against her sunny yellow tank top, and her blue denim shorts hugged sweetly curved hips above long, shapely legs. Her pretty brown hair was tied up on the top of her head in a no-nonsense style, but a few baby-fine wisps had escaped the knot to curl tightly against her long, slender neck.

His gaze shifted from those clinging, touchable curls to meet hers. Her serious eyes were darker than he remembered, and as they met his, a slight smile lit the soft gray depths. She had a great smile. Slow to appear but definitely worth waiting for, it revealed pretty, white teeth and a shallow dimple in her cheek. She looked, he decided, smiling back with growing satisfaction, much more welcoming than she had the other day.

But her welcoming look faded when she noticed the dog's absence.

"Where's Puppy?" she immediately demanded. She glanced beyond him to where he'd parked at the edge of the curb. Lifting her hand to shade her eyes from the late afternoon sunlight, she stared at the tinted windows. "Did you leave him in your truck?"

He shook his head. "No. At the house."

A slight frown drew her delicate eyebrows down. She held the door half-closed, as if barring him entrance. "You agreed to spend more time with him."

"Yeah, but I didn't agree to spend every waking moment with the animal. And I doubt he'd be much help moving boxes. He'd just be in the way."

Luc stepped forward, but she didn't move. "He wouldn't be in the way," she argued. "The more time you two spend together, the faster you'll bond, and the sooner this job will be done."

Luc set his back teeth. So much for his illusion of being welcomed. How could he have forgotten how single-minded she could be? Any other woman he knew would have been greeting him with open arms, thrilled, ecstatic, even—to have his company, his help, for the day. But not this one. Oh, no. All Miss Sigmund Freud of the canine community cared about was that overgrown mutt. He suggested dryly, "Maybe I should go back and get him."

She appeared to take the suggestion seriously. "No, I don't think so," she finally said, and grudgingly opened the door wider to allow him inside. "It would take too long, and I'm hoping we can pack up and go fairly quickly."

Luc was more than happy to pack up and go, and the quicker the better. He was halfway regretting he'd ever thought of this idea in the first place. Her attitude ticked him off. After all, this plan wasn't just benefiting him; it was helping her out, too.

Shrugging off his irritation, he entered her apartment. She'd already packed up everything; several cartons were stacked against the wall, all neatly labeled in black marker. Everything remaining appeared to be decorated in shades of beige. Beige walls. Beige carpet and sofa. Even beige cupboards and counter tops.

"You have something against color?" he asked.

Julie smiled a little. "No, but the landlord does. I guess he might have let me paint the walls in a pastel, but I just didn't get around to it." She glanced around the apartment. "The beige bothered my mother, too. We moved around a lot when I was kid—Dad was in the military—but no matter how short a time we stayed in a place, Mom always insisted on at least painting. She planned to do it for me here, but they moved before she had the chance."

"Your Dad's still on active duty?"

She shook her head. "Not my Dad, my brother. When he was transferred to Florida, my parents chose to follow him to be closer to him and his family. He has two little boys, ages one and two."

The faint wistfulness in her expression prompted him to ask, "But you didn't go along?"

She shook her head. "I couldn't. I'd just bought the institute."

Luc nodded. He could understand that. He headed towards her pile of boxes. He grasped the bottom of a large box marked Books and jiggled it experimentally, testing the weight.

"That's heavy," Julie said apologetically. "I shouldn't have put so many together—"

"No problem." Luc hefted it up on his shoulder. "I started out in the construction business. It gets you used to lifting and hauling. Just get the door, will you?"

She hurried to do so, and was grappling with another box when he returned. "Leave it," he ordered. "I'll do the carrying."

Julie shook her head. Luc might be bigger and stronger—much stronger, she realized, as he hoisted another big box of books onto his shoulder with an ease that secretly astounded her—but that didn't mean she expected him to do all the work. It was her stuff, after all. Besides, keeping busy helped hide the edginess she felt around him.

Because if she'd found him intimidating in her office, he seemed even more so today, dressed casually in a black T-shirt and faded Levi's. His big frame dominated her apartment, making it appear even tinier than it was. The well-worn Yankee baseball cap he had on—sacrilege of sacrilege in this West Coast city—should have given him a boyish air, especially when he twisted it around so the brim covered his strong, brown nape. It didn't. The cap, as well as the mirrored sunglasses that hid his eyes, merely emphasized the hard, chiseled planes of his lean cheeks and square jaw.

She tried not to watch him as they worked. It was surprisingly difficult. His strong body had an oddly compelling masculine grace. His jeans, so old that the stitching had whitened, couldn't disguise the strong, muscled thighs beneath the faded denim. The soft, worn material of his black T-shirt clung to the solid, sleek muscles of his broad shoulders and back, and stretched across a chest that looked impossibly wide compared to his lean waist and hips. The short sleeves revealed tanned, sinewy forearms and impressive biceps. Biceps that tightened and bulged every time he picked up a box.

When he paused to wipe off the sweat on his face with the edge of his T-shirt, she looked hastily away from his brown, washboard stomach. She'd seen handsomer men before, she reminded herself as they toted boxes out to his truck. Had even dated a few back in college when she'd had more time for a social life. She'd even seen men with better builds—although she couldn't remember who or when at the moment.

Nor could she remember anyone quite so bossy. Luc obviously wasn't happy about her helping. He kept demanding that she let *him* get that, before she hurt herself. But Julie loftily ignored his scowls and growls, hurrying as fast as she could, anxious to get finished and be on their way. She wanted to see Puppy—and escape Luc's disturbing presence.

"I'm not taking those," she said, when he started down her short hallway to retrieve the boxes he could see stacked in her small bedroom. "The landlord said since that room isn't being redone yet, I can leave what I want in there for a week or two until I rent a storage unit."

Luc stared at her, his hands on his hips. In his opinion, she didn't need a storage unit. There was plenty of room at the guesthouse for whatever she chose to store, and he didn't care how long she left it there.

He made the suggestion, adding as an afterthought, "Or you could leave it at my late aunt's house. I haven't put it on the market yet, and probably won't do so for a couple more months."

Julie shook her head. "Thank you, but they're fine here."

He didn't argue. He simply waited patiently for her to lock up the apartment, then strode down the sidewalk ahead of her to open the passenger door of his truck for her to climb in.

The high step reminded Julie of what she'd wanted to ask him. She gestured at the black leather seat, saying, "I saw you lift Puppy in the other day—from my office window," she added, as his dark brows rose inquiringly above his sunglasses. "Is he hurt? Does he have a hip or back injury?"

Luc shook his head. "No, I had the vet check him out right after my aunt died. Made sure his shots were up to date. Nothing's wrong with him at all."

Julie's smooth brow creased in puzzlement. "So why didn't you let him jump in himself?"

"He can't. He can jump down but not up. It must be too high for him. From the first time I picked him up at my aunt's, he refuses to even try. He just sits there until I lift him in. Speaking of which…" He stepped toward her. "Let me help you up."

He put his hands on her waist, preparing to pick her up, but Julie stepped hastily away, escaping from his warm grasp. "Thank you, I can manage," she said politely.

Luc shrugged, then moved aside. Julie took a deep breath. It *was* a high truck. Aware of Luc watching her, she stepped closer and put one foot up on the floor board, then grasped the top of the seat and the edge of the door. She gave a little bounce to hoist herself in. She didn't make it.

Luc moved closer. "Here. I'll just—"

"No. I can do it," she insisted, waving him away. Then she gritted her teeth and tried again, putting more oomph into it this time. She almost made it—she was halfway up—when she suddenly started to fall back.

A big hand settled on her rear end and hefted her the rest of the way up and in.

Julie almost scrambled across the seat to escape Luc's touch. The heat from his palm seemed to burn through her shorts, branding her bottom. Sitting upright, she turned to look down at him. All she could see in his mirrored sunglasses were twin reflections of her shocked face. The finely cut lips beneath the blasted things were set in a bland line, as unrevealing as the rest of his features. Still, she'd swear there was a hint of satisfaction in his deep voice as he said, "There you go," right before he shut the door.

Whistling faintly, Luc strode around to his side of the truck and climbed in. He started the ignition and pulled out into the traffic, then slanted a glance at Julie. Her cheeks were pink, and her spine was stiff. She'd folded her arms defensively across her chest as she stared straight ahead out the window.

Apparently, she wasn't inclined to talk. Luc was fine with that. He appreciated a woman who didn't feel the need to yap in his ear every second. He also appreciated a woman with a firm, round bottom, he thought, a smile tugging at the corner of his mouth. Though he seriously doubted Miss Prim Personified would appreciate his appreciation.

They might have made the entire trip in silence, but Luc's curiosity awoke as they passed house after house posted with For Sale signs.

"A lot of property changing hands in the area?" he asked after they passed an older, mission-style home with a big red sign planted on its front lawn.

She nodded, relaxing a bit as she tucked a loose strand of hair behind her ear. Her profile looked somber as she turned her head to gaze out the side window. "Prices have gone up so much these past few months, that it almost makes it crazy for the longtime residents to stay." The corners of her mouth turned down in a wry movement as she added, "Wealthy investors keep buying up whatever they can, tearing down the old houses and apartment buildings and putting up expensive condominiums. Most of the people in my building are going to have to move out of the area, since even rental prices around here have gotten so steep. But what do the greedy developers care as long they make a profit?"

He didn't reply. With a sigh, she shook off her melancholy and turned away from the window to face him. In a determinedly brighter voice, she asked, "So, you mentioned you started in construction. What kind of business are you in now?"

"Real estate. Investment and development." Feeling her stiffen beside him, he glanced at her. "Yeah, you got it right," he drawled. "I'm one of those greedy bastards you just mentioned."

Julie folded her hands in her lap. "I didn't call them bastards," she corrected him stiffly.

They both maintained a prudent silence as Luc turned onto the private road leading up the hill to his house.

The palm trees planted on both sides of the narrow road created a green canopy overhead. Fading sunlight flickered through the windows, filtering through the broad, fan-like leaves. Luc studied the palms as he drove past, automatically checking to see if they'd need pruning this year, then looked over at his passenger. The dappled light played over her serious expression and he wondered if she was regretting staying with him, what she'd think of his place.

He'd bought the property more than ten years ago for a solid sum of money. Real estate in southern California had already been on the rise, but if it hadn't been for its close proximity to his late aunt's home, he would have passed this place by. Even then he'd preferred to invest in property outside the state and, better yet, outside the country, for the best return on his money.

But except for various third and fourth cousins scattered throughout Italy, he'd been Aunt Sophia's only remaining relative, and he'd needed to be close enough to check in on her on a regular basis. Her house was less than fifteen minutes away, in a less expensive, more family-oriented, but still exclusive part of the city. When she'd died, he'd considered putting his place on the market along with hers. So far, he hadn't gotten around to listing either property—but he certainly planned to do so once he'd gotten rid of the damn dog she'd saddled him with.

Still, although his house wasn't his first choice of style, it suited him for now. It had been built in the art deco style during the Thirties by a prosperous producer of silent movies who'd wanted a home to impress his peers. Personally, Luc preferred a more modern design, or a warm, clean Mediterranean style like his aunt's house, similar to a villa he'd once bought and resold in Italy. But he was adaptable, and the designer and landscape architect he'd hired had done a good job with this property, retaining enough of the original character of the building to please future buyers hoping to own a bit of "old Hollywood," yet updating the amenities and playing down the decor enough to suit his tastes.

He stopped the truck by the metal box in front of the gates to key in a code, then pulled forward again as the iron security gates smoothly slid open.

Julie straightened in her seat beside him, her eager gaze fixed on the view beyond the truck's window as they headed up the long driveway. "What a wonderful yard! Such a wide green lawn and beautiful lilies!"

Luc slanted a glance at her. Any other female he knew would have been commenting on the huge house up ahead, exclaiming over the curved sweeping lines of blended stucco and glass. But not this one. Oh, no. Already he knew enough about Miss Canine Caretaker to bet it was images of dogs—more specifically, one overgrown mastiff—cavorting on that lush, manicured lawn that brought such a sparkle of delight to her expression.

Sure enough, she said, "Puppy must love this," her

eyes turning dreamy as she looked out the truck window at the thick grass on either side of the long, curving driveway. "Does he run around out here a lot?"

Luc didn't bother to beat around the bush—and he didn't allow the dog to, either. At least, not in the front yard. "The dog stays in the backyard," he told her bluntly.

"But there's all this room...."

"There's plenty of room in the back, too. And fewer plants for him to dig or chew up."

She didn't reply to that. She didn't say anything until he'd parked, when she thanked him politely as he helped her down from the high seat. She started to pull out one of the boxes from the bed of the truck, but Luc told her to leave it for the moment. "Let me show you around the main house before we unload," he said, and led the way to the front door. "It's easier to get to the guesthouse this way, rather than going around to the side."

He unlocked the door and let her inside, curious to see her reaction. The other women he'd brought here had certainly been impressed. Leila especially had gushed over the house and furnishings during their mercifully short affair every time she came over. But although Julie made polite remarks about the etched glass windows in the foyer, and glanced approvingly at the big mahogany clock they passed in the hallway, as they continued with a brief tour of the main rooms, Luc gained the impression she really didn't like his house.

He was right; Julie didn't like it. Oh, the architecture was interesting, and the furnishings tasteful—and obviously expensive—but the general impression was one of sterile coldness. The place felt more like a movie set than a home. Shiny chrome chairs, a white carpet.

Artwork obviously chosen to match the decor. In her opinion, the slick, cool lines of the interior didn't seem to fit Luc at all. Watching him pace through the rooms was rather like watching a wolf prowl through a museum. An interesting but odd juxtaposition. Not his natural habitat at all.

And if Luc seemed out of place, she kept thinking in dismay, then how would Puppy ever fit in?

But then Luc led her through another arched hallway to what he called the "family room." Not a family room, Julie thought, her tension easing as she stepped through double doors onto a carpet so thick her feet sank an inch into the pile. Luc's lair. His den.

Because here, finally, was a room that suited him. An unabashedly masculine room. The lush, hunter green carpet and softly gleaming mahogany paneling gave the impression of entering a forest. Off to the right was a doorway leading into a smaller room—obviously a home office—but Julie only spared a glance at the state-of-the-art equipment lined up on the long built-in counters and granite desk. Instead, her gaze was drawn to the art hung against the rich wood walls in the larger room. The paintings were stark, yet sophisticated—uncompromising in their color and intensity. A small, colorful Picasso. A tightly disciplined T. Novy grid. A free-flowing, sensuous Kaufman. A Douglas. A Simon. All in all, a small but eclectic collection she sensed instinctively Luc had chosen himself.

His taste in art surprised her. The entertainment unit he'd chosen was no surprise, however. Only a man would buy a television that big, Julie thought in faint amusement as she glanced toward the flat-screen dominating one wall of the room. She looked beyond it to a broad fireplace which filled another wall, and to the bookcase beside that. Then her gaze fell on the back of the leather sofa.

The sofa had to be the one that he'd mentioned in her office, Julie decided. The one he'd paid a ridiculous amount for. Even from behind, the piece looked expensive. Rich, dark brown leather was stretched over a frame that, with its curved back and broad, clawed feet, had an animalistic quality. She came around the side to see the front better—and gasped, her eyes widening in shock.

The whole center of the piece had been ripped open. Huge mounds of batting and down spilled forth from the wound, resembling nothing so much as a disemboweled animal.

"When you told me Puppy had chewed it I thought you meant he'd gnawed on an arm or a leg—but this! This is terrible! What was he doing?" Julie asked, her expression aghast as she met Luc's gaze. She glanced around the room. "Did he bother anything else?"

Luc shook his head. "Nope. Just this. I figure he worked on it for at least a couple hours."

Julie nodded in bewildered agreement, and more strands of hair tumbled free of the knot, to curl against her cheeks. She brushed them back, frowning back down at the sofa. "It would seem so...but I can't understand it. You'd think he'd start with an arm...or a leg. But he went right for the middle—as if he were attacking it."

"Yeah. Looks that way to me, too," Luc drawled. Hands on hips, he studied Julie's concerned expression, perversely pleased by her reaction. Finally she realized just what kind of a hellhound Puppy really was. What she'd be up against. What *he'd* been up against.

Then she sighed. "Poor Puppy."

Luc stiffened. "Poor *Puppy?* What are you talking about? Believe me, the couch didn't fight back."

She glanced at him in surprise. "No, but he had to be terribly upset to do something like this. His mind—his emotional psyche—must be all confused. Thank goodness we're here to help him."

"Yeah, thank goodness for that."

"Like you said," Julie added, ignoring his sarcastic tone, "it must have taken him hours. I'm just thankful he didn't eat some of that stuffing and get sick." She glanced up at Luc with a small frown. "Which reminds me, what are you feeding him?"

"Dog food."

She stared at him.

He sighed. "I suppose you want to see it."

Of course she did. They made their way into the huge old kitchen. Julie didn't comment on the pressed tin ceiling, or the gleaming, decorative tile work in the room. Or on the Italian marble floors, or the red vintage stove. All she cared about was checking Puppy's food.

"It's in here." Luc opened the cupboard beneath the sink. He picked up one of the cans stored there and handed it to her. "He gets this, mixed with some dry."

"Twice a day?"

"Once."

"He should be fed morning and night," she said firmly.

Luc stared down at her, his jaw tightening. "Fine. I'll have the housekeeper come in daily…"

His voice trailed off. Julie was shaking her head. "No. *You* need to feed him, Luc." She was adamant. "Not the housekeeper. It will help him—"

"I know, I know." Luc held up his hand to stop her. "It will help Puppy's and my relationship."

She rewarded him with an approving look. "That's

right." She read the label and added, "And this brand is fine, as long as you give him fresh cooked meat now and again, and definitely some vegetables."

Luc leaned against the counter, folding his arms across his chest. "Maybe I should have the gardener start a vegetable patch out back for the dog."

"There's an idea," she said, her expression brightening.

Yeah, the woman definitely had a one-track mind, Luc decided. He was glad she liked the dog—hell, he was *counting* on her liking the animal enough to take him permanently. But she didn't have to think about Puppy all the time. Nor be so damned *dog*matic about what she thought was good for the mastiff.

Because when you got right down to it, the dog was just that: a dog. Not a hairy, big-eyed orphan left on Luc's doorstep. Still, if she was determined to believe Puppy was some poor, misunderstood animal, who was he to stop her?

Abruptly, he straightened away from the counter. "Let's go see the guesthouse. And poor little Puppy."

She was all for that. She was right on his heels as he led her back through the hallway and out the French doors that led to the covered patio. The guesthouse was beyond the pool, and, as Luc expected, Puppy was lying by his crate on the guesthouse patio.

Luc pointed in the dog's direction. "There he is."

Julie's face lit up. "Puppy!" she called. "Come here, boy!"

"He won't come," Luc warned.

Of course, the dog made a liar out of him. After staring intently at them for a few seconds across the wide span of lawn, Puppy rose, then came toward them at a restrained trot.

For such a big, brutal-looking animal, Puppy was

oddly graceful in motion, Luc silently admitted to himself. The dog's huge feet hit the ground lightly, and his muscles coiled and uncoiled in a smooth rhythm. He came to a stop about ten feet away, then walked slowly straight to Julie, cropped ears flattened placatingly and big brown eyes gazing up at her.

He accepted her petting with dignified excitement, his stubby tail wagging in polite response. And when she spoke to him, Luc was surprised to hear a deep answering whimper rumble from the dog's big chest. The mastiff acted as if he'd just found a new best friend.

Luc, he completely ignored.

Julie wasn't paying him any attention, either. She kept stroking the dog, crooning what a "good boy" he was. Luc stood there a few minutes, watching Julie fuss over the mastiff, watching Puppy lap it up.

It wasn't until Luc finally said, "We'd better go check out the guesthouse and unload before it gets dark," that Julie seemed to remember he was around.

"Yes, let's," she agreed, giving Puppy's big head a final pat.

They headed toward the guesthouse with Puppy trotting between them. The dog followed her in when Luc opened the door, flopping down on the hardwood floor as if he had a perfect right to be there. He didn't move as Luc showed her around the space—complete with a small sitting room, bathroom and bedroom.

"There's no kitchen—just a small kitchenette with a microwave and coffeemaker," Luc pointed out. "But you're welcome to use the kitchen at the main house whenever you want. I never use it."

"Never?" she asked, startled.

"Except for coffee sometimes in the mornings," Luc admitted. "Beyond that, I don't cook."

"I see." For some reason, she appeared to find that interesting. He watched her, wondering what was behind her thoughtful expression now. Whatever it was, she didn't share it but simply thanked him for the offer before heading back to the truck to unload her stuff.

Puppy waited in the guesthouse as they made numerous trips back forth, taking a nap beside the door. The unloading didn't take much time at all. After Luc had set the final carton down, he stretched, twisting this way and that to ease the muscles in his back.

Then he turned—to find Julie watching him.

He lifted his brow. She hastily looked away. And then she met his eyes again, her usual serious expression on her face. "Thank you, Luc." She gestured around the small sitting room, at her boxes stacked neatly to the side. Her voice soft with sincerity, she added, "I honestly believe this is going to work out well for all of us."

"Yeah," Luc agreed, looking down into her pretty eyes. More of her hair had come loose from the knot now, to fall around her neck and shoulders in casual disarray. She looked slightly flushed, her cheeks pink from the effort of moving all her boxes. A smear of dust marked one high cheekbone.

She didn't look standoffish now. She looked warm and rumpled and a little tired from all the moving. Sexy and cuddly, her skin dewy and glowing from her exertions. He wanted to reach out, run a finger along her smooth, damp skin; instead, he flexed his fingers, then tucked them safely in his back pockets, away from temptation.

He'd ask her out to dinner, Luc decided. He had a lot of work to get through this evening, but he could take the time to go out with her. Get to know her a little better. After all, he reasoned, they were practically living together now.

Then Julie looked over at Puppy, flopped out on his side, snoring lightly. Her expression softened even more. "Does he usually sleep in here?"

Luc looked at the dog, too. "No, out on the side patio. In his dog crate."

"I'd like to see it," Julie said.

Puppy got up and followed as Luc led her out the door and around the corner of the small building. The crate was tucked against the wall beneath a trellis roof built over the small patio.

"Does he sleep out here all the time?" Julie asked, studying the big, plastic kennel, with Puppy at her side.

Luc nodded. "Yeah—he wants to," he added to forestall the protest he see from her expression was coming. "He goes in and out of it as he pleases and he slept in the crate at my aunt's, too. Only she kept it in the kitchen."

"But you don't."

"No. I don't."

He injected as much finality as he could into his tone, and it must have worked. Julie didn't argue, but thoughtfully studied his set expression for a second.

"Well, that's fine for now," she finally said. "The weather's still warm, after all. By the time it gets colder, maybe things will have changed."

They certainly would, Luc thought grimly. By then, he didn't plan to have the dog around at all. He'd have fulfilled his promise to his aunt, and once again would be free of responsibility.

When Luc remained silent, Julie looked down at Puppy, who'd edged his big frame between the humans and his crate. Unable to help herself, she reached out to stroke his broad head. The dog looked up at her with what seemed to be a wistful expression.

There was a danger here, Julie realized, looking down into his big brown eyes. One she hadn't foreseen when she'd agreed to this plan. The danger that she'd become too attached to Puppy—would step in to give him attention and affection, instead of waiting for Luc to do so.

So, with a final pat, she stepped back, saying, "Well, I'd better go start unpacking."

She started to turn away, and Luc put out his hand to stop her, lightly catching hold of her upper arm. "Why don't we go out and get a bite to eat first?" he said. "I have about an hour or two I can spare before I get down to work."

Julie looked up at him. He'd pushed his sunglasses up on his forehead. This close, she could feel his body heat, see the fine lines etched in the corners of his heavy-lidded eyes and the golden specks in his brown irises. His lean fingers tightened slightly on her arm, and she felt the tautness in his muscles as he watched her intently, awaiting her answer.

A corresponding tension made her stomach swoop— as if she were suddenly on a runaway roller coaster. Her heart jumped and her breathing quickened. Her palms grew damp. She was much too aware of him—she didn't want to be aware of him. Of the way his lips set in a straight line. Of the slightly crooked bump in his masculine nose and how sturdy his neck looked. Of the wide span of his shoulders and the sinewy strength of his forearms. Of the heat of his fingers on her sensitive skin.

Animal magnetism, she thought in vague wonder. She'd heard the term before, but she'd never believed it really existed.

Now she knew it did. Because Luc Tagliano had it

in spades. And that was another danger she hadn't expected. That she'd be attracted to a man who wasn't her type at all.

She knew what type of man she wanted to eventually marry. A man who wanted what she wanted—a stable home, a family, a loving, lasting relationship.

Luc Tagliano couldn't even commit to owning a dog.

And if she wanted to change that, she needed to direct his attention back where it belonged. On Puppy.

She drew a deep breath. The faint, musky scent of his skin and tangy aftershave drifted toward her—an expensive-smelling aftershave that had no doubt been given to him by one of his girlfriends. She slowly exhaled…then took a cautious step backward, gently breaking his grip on her arm.

His eyes narrowed. She felt as if she were inching away from a wild animal who was preparing to pounce.

His eyes narrowed more when she said, her voice slightly husky, "No, thank you." She cleared her throat, then gestured at Puppy, who was watching them with his ears up and his head tilted to the side. "If you only have a little extra time today, then maybe it would be better if you spent it with Puppy. Getting in the daily socializing you promised to do."

Luc scowled. He put his hands on his hips. "Socializing? What does that mean?"

"It means you need to talk to the dog, Luc. Get to know him better. Don't forget, you have basic training class to attend with him again tomorrow."

With that final piece of advice, she turned and headed back toward the guesthouse.

Hands still on his hips, Luc stood there watching Julie walk away, Puppy by his side. With his brooding gaze fixed on her departing figure, he said in an annoyed growl, "Talk to the dog? That woman is just full of crazy ideas. Who does she think I am? Dr. Dolittle?"

Julie disappeared into the guesthouse, and Luc's jaw tightened. He glanced at the mastiff, adding, "What does she think will happen if I talk to you? That you'll suddenly start talking back?"

Puppy obviously had no intention of talking back. He moved in front of his crate, blocking it with his body. Then he laid down, watching Luc intently.

Julie's whole attitude irritated Luc. He started pacing, shooting narrow-eyed glances at the guesthouse door even though she could no longer be seen. "She's the damnedest woman I've ever met," he muttered, then scowled down at the dog. "In her eyes, *you* can do no wrong. Even ripping up my couch is just an 'upset' on your part, a small problem with your delicate dog psyche. A minor, seven-thousand-dollar mistake."

The mastiff glanced away from Luc's accusing stare to focus on a small black beetle, scuttling along the sidewalk.

Luc kept pacing. "She's as animal-crazy and stubborn as Aunt Sophia used to be."

The dog's ears pricked forward. He lifted his head. His small whimper drew Luc's attention.

Luc paused, and the beetle scuttled off to safety in the grass. "See, even you agree," he said, giving Puppy an approving glance. "Well, get plenty of rest. We've got that damn training class to attend tomorrow."

His mouth tightened at the thought. He left, striding across the lawn into the house, while Puppy went into his crate to lie there alone, awake and on guard through the night.

Chapter Four

Teaching your pet to play nicely:

Don't let that that handsome, hairy face sway
you. Proper training is an absolute necessity when
acquiring a new pet. One-on-one training is all
well and good for a start, but group classes are the
perfect way to teach your animal to socialize better. He'll lap up the experience—and so will you!

Just remember: the smarter they are, the harder
they are to train.
Basic Training 101, Dr. M.T. Yessuh

The trainer was watching them.

"Okay, this is it," Luc said from the corner of his
mouth. "If you don't want Ms. Iron Maiden to come
over here again, for God's sake get it right this time.
Sit!"

Puppy glanced up at him, then looked away, remaining on his feet.

Even from across the institute training grounds, Luc could see the sunlight glinting on her glasses as her gimlet-eyed gaze swung their way. Urgently, he said, "Sit, damn it! Sit! Ah, hell, here she comes."

Ms. Irenmadden bore down on them, striding rapidly past the twenty or so owners and their obedient dogs, all lined up in a regular pooch parade.

The trainer chugged to a halt in front of Luc. She jabbed her glasses up higher on her pug nose, then planted her capable hands on her broad hips and glared at him. "Do we have a problem here, Mr. Tagliano?"

"No, we don't—the dog does. He doesn't want to sit."

"Then *correct* him, Mr. Tagliano." She twitched the leash out of Luc's hand, then barked "Sit!" while simultaneously squeezing the area above the mastiff's haunches.

Puppy sat.

Ms. Irenmadden sniffed in triumph. "Now you try it." She handed the leash back to Luc.

Luc barked the command and pressed.

Puppy sat.

"There. He did it!" the trainer declared, as if Luc couldn't see for himself. Grimly satisfied, she moved away, her vigilant gaze zeroing in on a spaniel sniffing at a dandelion in the grass. "No, no! Mr. Henderson! Frederick needs to focus! Now let's all practice sitting again."

Luc gave the command along with the others and Puppy sat—but not without the added squeeze on his haunches. Aware of the other owners' amused or condescending gazes, Luc tried again. And again. But Puppy only cooperated under pressure.

"What's wrong with you?" Luc asked in exasperation, meeting the dog's unreadable brown gaze. "You know this. You sailed through basic training with flying colors according to Aunt Sophia."

Puppy's cropped ears pricked forward.

An older, white-haired woman standing next to them, leaned toward Luc. Pursing her bright pink lips in disapproval, she said, "Now, don't scold him. You'll just make him feel bad." She added in a loud whisper, "It's not his fault he's not too bright. Mixed breeds just aren't as intelligent as purebred dogs."

Luc's jaw tightened. "He's not a mixed breed."

"No?" The woman looked at Puppy, her penciled eyebrows lifting, doubt written all over her plump face.

"No," Luc said. "He's Italian."

The woman's expression cleared. "Oh, *Italian*. That explains it. Italians are so—so Italian, don't you think? What with the Mob and the Pope and everything." She waved her stubby fingers in the air, making her diamond rings sparkle, the gesture encompassing—and dismissing—Italians and their dogs everywhere. "Believe me, shitzus—like my little Twinkle here—are much, much smarter than Italian dogs. He's an Oriental breed. Everyone knows Asians' IQs are higher than everyone else's."

Luc and Puppy both glanced down at the chubby, little snowball of a dog squatting at the end of the gold leash in the woman's hands. Despite the mildness of the weather, the animal was decked out in a pink sweater and had a pink bow clipped to the top of his head. The sweater had rolled up when the dog sat to accommodate the animal's round pink belly, which heaved with each panting breath he took.

The dog's tongue matched the sweater and bow, Luc

noticed. It also matched the pink pantsuit and high heels the woman had on, and her lipstick, as well.

"Isn't he *adorable?*" she exclaimed. Her pink lips stretched in a beaming smile as she looked down at her pet. "And so brilliant. I named him Twinkle because he's such a little star! Just watch what he can do. Get up, Twinkle! Get up for Mumsie!"

Twinkle wasn't inclined to get up—for Mumsie or anyone else. Although Luc suspected he'd move pretty quickly for a cookie or two. But finally, in response to repeated entreaties—and an especially forceful tug on the gold leash—the little dog reluctantly stood up on his short legs. All three inches of them.

"Now, sit, Twinkle!" the woman commanded.

Twinkle sat—before the words were even out of her mouth.

The woman gave a smug smile. "See? Isn't he clever?"

Puppy yawned.

Luc shrugged. "Or lazy. Judging by that belly, it looks like Tinkle does a lot of sitting around. You should have named him Buddha."

The woman bristled. "Are you calling my Twinkle fat?" Snatching up the little dog, she pressed her round cheek against the animal's. Two pairs of accusing eyes glared at him from beneath shaggy bangs, and two pairs of white heads quivered in disapproval. "How dare you!" the woman declared.

Twinkle stuck out his pink tongue.

Luc heaved a sigh. "Look, lady, why don't you and your little shitpoo just mind your own business and—"

"Is there a problem here?"

The question was the same one Ms. Irenmadden had

asked a few minutes earlier. But the soft voice was entirely different.

Luc turned to face Julie. He hadn't noticed her approaching, though he'd glimpsed her watching the class a while back from the rear door of the office building. She was dressed again in her blue shirt, complete with logo above her right breast, and paired this time with a dark blue skirt. Even in the bright daylight, her skin still looked smooth and creamy, still impossibly soft. And her gray eyes held a by now familiar reproving expression.

An expression Luc had seen just this morning, when he'd decided to feed Puppy the hamburger he'd brought home in a doggy bag the night before from his lonely dinner, rather than the mutt's canned chow.

Luc told her, "There's no problem—"

"Yes, there is!" the woman interrupted. "This man insulted me! He insulted Twinkle!"

"I'm sure he didn't intend to," Julie said.

Luc opened his mouth to correct her, but closed it again at the warning look in her eyes.

Julie patted the woman's plump arm soothingly. "Why don't you and Twinkle go over to see Ms. Irenmadden? She's moving on to the sit-stay command with the more advanced members of the class, and I think Twinkle might be ready."

"He certainly is!" the woman declared. She glared at Luc one last time, then set Twinkle on his short legs. With a tug on the leash, she tottered off in the trainer's direction, her high heels sinking into the lawn with each step and the little dog trailing behind her.

"Teacher's pet," Luc growled.

Julie sighed, and glanced up at him. "Can't you behave? Did you have to start a fight with her?"

"Me! She's the one who started it, insulting Italians and their weird ways and all." He shook his head. "Like she should talk. What kind of woman dresses up her dog, and wears clothes to match?"

Julie took a deep breath. "Bitsy Wellington—"

"Bitsy?" Luc snorted.

Julie soft lips tightened. "Bitsy Wellington is wealthy," she persisted, "but she's also very lonely. All the money in the world can't buy Bitsy the love she gets from that little shitzu. I'm not surprised that she's defensive of Twinkle."

Luc scowled. Julie made him feel guilty—and he didn't like it. "Well, it can't be healthy," he growled. "The way she dresses him up and all. Especially in pink."

Julie tilted her head to consider the matter. Her hair slid over her shoulder with the movement, the silky brown strands glinting in the sunlight. "I don't know," she said slowly, "The way I see it, every minute that Bitsy spends thinking about Twinkle is one less minute she spends thinking about herself. Until she got the dog, she spent most of her time in bed, suffering from imaginary illnesses. Anyway," she continued more briskly. "Bitsy isn't the problem here. You are. Why does Ms. Irenmadden have to keep coming over to help you with the sit command?"

Luc's scowl deepened. "That tattletale—"

Casting her eyes towards heaven for help, Julie said, "She didn't tell me, Luc. For goodness sake, I could see her talking with you from across the yard. Aren't you getting it?"

"Like I keep telling everyone, *I'm* getting it—it's the dog who doesn't have a clue." Luc pointed at Puppy. "He simply refuses to sit on command. I have to press his haunches every time."

"Are you sure your aunt put him through basic training?"

"She told me she had and that he did great. That he passed effortlessly—and believe me, Aunt Sophia never lied."

"Hmm." Julie looked at Puppy, who met her gaze with a faint wag of his stubby tail. "Maybe we've been giving the wrong commands. *Siedasi!*" she said in Italian.

Puppy sat.

Luc stared at the mastiff. "Well, I'll be—"

"*Indichi!*" Julie commanded.

Puppy laid down.

"*Alzis!*"

Puppy rose immediately to his feet.

"Well, what do you know," Luc said slowly. "He responds to Italian. How on earth did you figure that out?"

Julie's slender shoulders lifted in a faint shrug. "You said your family's Italian. That you spoke it and your aunt loved anything Italian. Since Georgia had told me he wasn't responding, I decided to look up a few commands to try out. It just made sense."

Yeah, it did. Luc stared down at the mastiff. His aunt had used her native language whenever the opportunity presented itself. So why hadn't he thought she might use it on the dog? "*Siedasi. Indichi. Alzis!*" he commanded—and Puppy responded perfectly each time.

Julie smiled. "Good dog." She gave Puppy an approving scratch behind the ears. "Looks like your aunt trained him well."

"Yeah." Luc met Puppy's innocent brown gaze. "I guess she did."

Julie headed off then, moving down the line to pet a

frisky terrier here, a sober Doberman there. The sun behind her cast a glow on her slender figure, sparkling in
her brown hair while the light breeze flirted with the
hem of her skirt, furling it around her sexy legs. Luc
watched as she gracefully crouched down by the youn-
gest member of the class, a silky black Labrador puppy
that eagerly clambered into her lap to try to lick her
face. Julie laughingly tilted her chin up to avoid the canine kisses, then wrapped her arms around the pup to
give him a hug. After a brief cuddle, she rose again.
Tucking her hair behind her ear, she chatted briefly
with the owner—a middle-aged guy in a Hawaiian
shirt—then finally left the group to head back to her office.

Luc's gaze remained fixed on her as she strode past
the track and obstacle course, subconsciously register-
ing the graceful sway of her slim hips. But superim-
posed on her slender figure was the image in his mind
of his skinny, straight-backed great aunt, dressed in the
inevitable black she'd worn since the day her husband
had died forty years earlier.

Luc remembered one of the last times he'd visited
her. He'd ended up confiding some of his frustrations
with a new crew he'd been working with on a major
project out of state.

His aunt had leaned toward him from her high-
backed wing chair. She patted his arm gently, her small,
arthritic hands encased in her Sunday-best, black silk
gloves. "Speak to them more kindly, Lucien," she'd
told him, in the Italian she'd loved so well. "Sometimes it's not what you say, but the manner in which you
say it that is important. Practice patience, my nephew.
Not every problem is so quickly solved."

But this problem had been. By Julie.

His gaze narrowed on her as she opened the door to the building and disappeared inside. In less than five minutes, she'd discovered why Puppy wasn't responding. Somehow she'd realized something that he should have known right off, but hadn't.

And that bothered him.

Chapter Five

Learning to obey simple commands:

Leashes and collars are handy to have, but when teaching your pet to obey simple commands, there is one tool that is absolutely essential:

The sausage.

Nothing reinforces good behavior faster in an animal's mind than a delicious treat in his stomach. Combine praise with the treat, and you're more than halfway to your goal of owning a perfectly behaved pet.

Perfecting Pet Etiquette, Rayna Ritaville

Lots of things bothered Luc during the next week. To begin with, as he'd sensed when he'd first shown her around the place, Julie wasn't all that impressed with his house. And she was obviously determined to transform the place into a perfect home before she moved on.

That is, the perfect home for Puppy.

Luc caught the first scent of her scheme early Monday morning as he was leaving for work. He'd just knotted his tie and picked up his briefcase, when a delicious odor caught his attention. Lifting his head, he sniffed the air. Eggs? Hash browns? Toast? Definitely coffee. And—could it be?—Italian sausage frying?

The mere possibility made his mouth water. Setting down his briefcase, he followed his nose into the kitchen.

There he found Julie, standing in front of the red vintage stove he'd never used. She was dressed for work in her blue shirt and pants. Puppy was sitting close by her side.

Both glanced Luc's way as he entered. Puppy quickly returned his yearning gaze to the stove. But Julie gave Luc a slow, sweet smile.

"Good morning." She gestured with the spatula she was holding at the frying pan. "I've already eaten and there's still plenty left. Do you have time for breakfast?"

Luc didn't. He planned to make five or six phone calls before noon and go over the initial bids on the Costa Rica project with his lawyer, as well.

But somehow, he found himself loosening his tie and sitting at the table. And chowing down the best home-cooked breakfast he'd had since he'd moved out of his aunt's house more than thirteen years ago.

They started talking, idly at first—Luc's attention was definitely more on the juicy sausage and scrambled eggs she'd prepared than chitchat. They talked about the beautiful weather. How Julie was settling in. Puppy's progress in training class.

Then—Luc wasn't quite sure how it happened—the conversation turned to the way he'd decorated his house. In relation to Puppy, of course.

"I didn't decorate it," he protested, looking across the table at Julie who had sat ostensibly "just to finish her coffee" while he ate. "I hired a designer—an expensive interior designer—to do it." He bit down on his toast.

"And it looks expensive," Julie said. "But it's certainly not 'dog-friendly.' For goodness sake, it's barely people-friendly." She leaned toward him with an earnest expression on her face. "I know you didn't have a dog then, but seriously, Luc, what were you thinking? Putting a white carpet in your living room. And those chairs. Chrome may look great, but who can relax on them?"

Luc forked some eggs into his mouth and scowled at her as he chewed. After swallowing, he said, "I didn't buy those chairs to relax in. They're an investment."

She set down her cup. "I know, and I understand that. But it's your home as well as a showplace, isn't it?"

"Yeah. So?"

"So it should be comfortable."

"I'm comfortable enough."

"But Puppy isn't. And it's his home now, too. You want him to feel comfortable here, don't you?"

Luc didn't give a damn if the dog was comfortable or not. In fact, he didn't want the hound digging in at all when he'd be leaving so soon. But Luc also knew that if he said so—admitted what he had planned—he'd just be in for a lot of grief.

So he ate a little faster, then tried a different tack. "Puppy has a comfortable bed out in his crate—"

"Which is outside. In the cold and dark. All alone."

"He's a dog, damn it! I'm sure he loves to be outside. So he can do dog things. Like run around. And—" He paused, trying to think of another dog activity. "And sniff."

"Of course he likes to be outside," Julie agreed in a patient tone that made him sound like the unreasonable one. "Sometimes. He also likes to come indoors, too. Puppy needs family time just as much as a human does. Not only are dogs domesticated, they're pack animals. They want to spend time with their pack, which, in Puppy's case, is you. You aren't planning on sitting with him outside by his crate each night, are you?"

Hell, no, he wasn't planning on that. Luc opened his mouth to destroy that misconception, but before he could, she added in a meaningful tone, "Because I'm sure you haven't forgotten you promised to spend time with Puppy each night."

Luc frowned. Damn. He had forgotten.

He glanced at Puppy, who'd come over to sit beside him. The mastiff watched him expectantly, liquid brown eyes following Luc's every move as he ate. The dog didn't look as if he were suffering in Luc's opinion. In fact, since Julie had joined their little menagerie, Luc would swear the mastiff had an extra wag in his stubby tail.

Luc told Julie so, while slipping a piece of sausage to the dog, who wagged right on cue—

"You shouldn't encourage him to beg, Luc," Julie said reproachfully.

Luc slanted a glance her way. She'd put her elbows on the table and had her chin propped on her hands. All the better to level her unwavering gray gaze on him. Her big eyes were as expectant as Puppy's. But she wasn't hoping for a handout—oh, no, not her. She was after bigger game. She wanted Luc's complete capitulation on the issue of Puppy coming inside during the evenings.

Luc tried to fight it. He ate. He argued. He ate. He growled. He ate—then finally sighed, unable to eat anymore. Tilting his chair back on two legs, he patted his flat stomach, feeling replete. Then he conceded the argument. Because, damn it, she was right. He'd given his word to spend time with Puppy.

And besides, the food made him mellow.

So, with a lot of halfhearted grumbling that Julie and Puppy loftily ignored, Luc left for work—late—where he rearranged his schedule of business meetings so he could be home in the evenings. And, because she was also right in assuming he didn't plan to spend the time with the dog outside, crouched down by the animal's crate, the gutted sofa was sent out to be reupholstered. Within a few days it was returned. Newly redone, it sprawled again before the fireplace with not a scratch on the dark, rich leather remaining as evidence of Puppy's perplexing attack.

After the couch had been returned, it became a habit for Luc and Julie—and Puppy, of course—to spend a couple hours in the den each evening after a home-cooked meal. Julie persuaded Luc to watch a couple of dog-training videos, and another about *Cane corso* mastiffs. Luc wouldn't admit it, but Julie suspected he'd liked that one. His dark eyes had gleamed as he watched the reenactment of Roman warriors riding into battle with the mastiffs at their sides. Puppy watched them, too, his head tilted to the side as his gaze tracked the dogs racing across the screen.

But usually they watched sports or the evening news, with Luc inevitably sprawled at one end of the couch, while Julie curled up in the other corner. Puppy, after a sneaky attempt to claim the middle—a bid gently discouraged by Julie, and much more vehemently by Luc—finally appropriated a spot on the carpet in front of the fire. There he'd nap, snoring stentoriously, awakening occasionally to give a sleepy, warning "woof" at the cats cavorting in commercials or in response to the ringing of the phone in the nearby office.

At first, the phone rang a lot. Luc had two land lines, both used for business, and a cell phone, as well. No one called on the cell phone. Luc reserved that for outgoing calls. But his business lines rang constantly. After a couple of nights of the disturbance, he usually set both lines on silent mode, but when he forgot, voices would erupt in the room. American voices, foreign accented voices, leaving messages about profits, losses, updates on building codes, fees—and other business specifics that Julie didn't understand.

Sometimes female voices would drift over the machine, inviting Luc to dinner, to the theater, to "just come over"—*to go to bed,* was how Julie mentally completed those particular messages.

She was grateful to those disembodied voices. They reminded her not to become too used to spending lazy evenings with Luc. To joking, and talking, and getting to know him. Not to become too attached to the beast.

So, when Puppy's daily "social hour" ended each night, Julie retired to the guesthouse, Puppy to his kennel and Luc to his home office where he worked late into the night.

If Luc considered his present work schedule as "cutting back," Julie couldn't imagine what his life had been like before he had assumed the care of the mastiff. He left before six each morning and didn't return until after six each night. Once or twice a week he'd come in late, blandly ignoring Julie's evident but un-spoken disapproval. His disposition in some ways re-minded Julie of a bloodhound. When he wasn't working, Luc could appear almost lazy. He played and teased and didn't seem to take much seriously. But when he focused on his work, he was like a blood-hound on the scent. Pushing past any obstacle, totally focused on his goal.

Julie worked long hours, too, but unfortunately not, she thought ruefully, with nearly so intent a focus or successful an outcome. Although the institute was out-wardly thriving, with more clients and classes than ever before, she kept slowly sinking into the red. Why or how, she couldn't discover. Animal behavior she under-stood. Business, she didn't. She needed to hire an ac-countant, she often thought worriedly, grappling with profits and losses, tax forms and personnel records. But the idea of adding yet another expense made her hesitate.

She pushed the problem to the back of her mind, dis-tracting herself with her work with the animals at the clinic, and—most especially—the training of Puppy and Luc. Puppy tugged at her heart; Luc kept her on her toes. The man made her wary, but he also made her laugh. And, oh, how she envied his energy. Like a Jack Russell ter-rier—on a much larger scale, of course—he never seemed to slow down. Every day, he got up at dawn to exercise, maintaining his impressive physique by working out in an exercise room located in the back of the house. When he'd been in construction, he'd told Julie, he used to get plenty of exercise on the job. Now, he lifted weights.

So, in order to install the next phase of her "Luc and Puppy Bonding" plan, Julie cornered him in his weight room a few days later.

Luc had left the sliding glass door open, probably to enjoy the dawn sunshine. Julie stepped inside, then froze.

Luc was naked.

Okay, not totally naked, she realized in the few seconds it took for her gaze to glide far enough down his broad brown back to notice the sweatpants hanging low on his lean hips. Still, he looked big and bare enough for a flush to rise in her cheeks.

He hadn't noticed her—he was sitting on his weight bench with his back to the door, drying his face with a white towel. A bit unnerved by so much muscular, gleaming brown flesh, Julie would have backed out again unseen, but Puppy had followed her in. She bumped into his big body with a muffled "oomph" that caused Luc to glance over his shoulder.

His dark brows lifted in surprise. "What's up?"

"Nothing. I— You just—" She took a deep breath, and straightened her spine, making an effort to regain her composure. With a dismissive wave of her hand, she tried to back out again, saying, "You're busy—I'll catch you later."

"No problem. I'm finished here." Luc turned, straddling the bench to face her. With his curious gaze fixed on her face, he casually rubbed the towel across his glistening brown chest, down his ridged abdomen and under his armpits, as he asked, "What did you need?"

Julie kept her gaze on his, refusing to let the white towel distract her. "I need—" What *did* she need? Her mind had gone blank. Trying to hide her consternation, her gaze dropped from his to fall on his equipment. His *gym* equipment. That was it. "I need to talk to you about exercising."

"Yeah? You want to use the weight machine?" His

gaze skimmed over her figure, clad in her working pants and shirt, with new interest. He tossed aside the towel. Picking up a black tank top, he stretched it across his arms, then slipped it smoothly over his head and down into place. "You might want to change first."

No longer confronted by so much bare male skin, Julie found it easier to articulate. "Actually, I wanted to talk to you about *Puppy's* exercise."

Luc eyed the dog, who'd managed to push past Julie and was sniffing cautiously at a huge barbell. "What about it?"

"He needs more exercise than he's getting." On sure ground once again, Julie added firmly, "You need to walk him daily, Luc."

"I don't see why—" Luc aimed his thumb at the window that framed the backyard "—when he has that huge yard to run around in."

"It's not enough. Walking provides other positive re-inforcements he can't get on his own. He needs to learn to follow you. To accept you as the leader, as well as be exposed to fresh sights and sounds and smells."

Luc shook his head. "I don't have time to walk him every day."

"I know," she conceded. "But on the days you don't, you can put him on the treadmill while you lift weights."

She could see Luc was intrigued by the suggestion. He glanced at the dog with grudging respect. "He can do that?"

Julie nodded. "We just have to teach him how. In slow steps."

She led Puppy over to the machine, giving him time to sniff it. Then, under Luc's interested gaze, she had Puppy step up on the machine, then she led him off again. She repeated the exercise, then slowly, carefully, turned the treadmill on.

After some minor hesitation, the big dog quickly caught the pace, and strode happily along, his tongue lolling out, his stub of a tail wagging smugly.

Julie clasped her hands together in delight. "He's a natural!"

Luc grunted in agreement.

Julie let Puppy walk a few minutes then carefully turned the machine off, and led the dog back down. "See? Nothing to it."

Luc remained silent.

She looked at him questioningly. "So what do you say?"

"I say okay," Luc conceded. "Puppy can come exercise with me."

Julie smiled. "Thanks, Luc."

Satisfied, she turned to go. She'd taken two steps to the door when a grasp on the back of her shirt jerked her to a halt.

"Not so fast. We haven't finished yet."

She glanced back in surprise. Luc was holding on to her shirt, keeping her in place.

He smiled, showing his white teeth and wolfish incisors. "He can exercise with me as long as I get what I want out of the deal."

Julie stopped smiling. She tugged her shirt out of his loosened grip and faced him with a frown. "And what do you want?"

Luc studied her expression, biting back another smile at the suspicion on her face. "I want you…" He paused deliberately, waited until her smoky eyes widened and her lips parted in surprise. Then, satisfied with her reaction, continued blandly, "To walk with us, too, sometime."

Julie's eyes narrowed at his teasing, then her lips curved into her slow smile. "Fine. You've got a deal." And she left, Puppy at her heels.

From then on, Luc put Puppy on the treadmill while he worked out in the mornings and walked the dog whenever he came home early enough, always insisting Julie come along. Julie really didn't mind. She needed the exercise, too, and trying to keep up with Luc's and Puppy's long strides gave her plenty. It wasn't long before Puppy's already impressive musculature became even more defined—and she trimmed off a few pounds, as well.

So, with the exercise situation resolved and less than half of the agreed-upon six weeks remaining, Julie turned her attention to another of Puppy's problems: his continuing tendency to destroy plants, stray shoes and expensive outdoor teak furniture—an unfortunate lapse on the dog's part that made Luc threaten to throw him into the pool.

She attacked the subject about a week after the exercise episode, catching Luc in the kitchen again before he left for work. He had on his tie, and in his hand was one of the freshly baked doughnuts she'd set out as bait to delay him.

He was on to her now, though. As soon as he saw her enter the kitchen, his brown eyes narrowed with suspicion. He crammed the rest of his doughnut into his mouth and picked up his coffee cup. "Gotta get going," he said thickly.

Julie stayed in the doorway to block his escape and got right to the point. "You need to take Puppy shopping, Luc."

"Shopping!" He frowned at her over his cup, then turned his scowl on Puppy, who'd followed her into the room. "That's it. This is where I draw the line. I'm not going to start dressing that dog up, I don't care what it would do for his tender psyche."

"Not for clothes," Julie said soothingly. "For toys. And dog chews. They're good for his teeth. I'm sure your aunt used to give him some." She remembered he'd once mentioned he hadn't yet sold his late aunt's property and, on a sudden inspiration, added, "If you don't want to go to the store, maybe you could stop by your aunt's house and pick up one of Puppy's old toys."

To her surprise, Luc's expression tightened. He turned away to set his cup in the sink with a sharp clatter. "I don't have time to go over there and poke around right now. I'll pick him up some new stuff."

Julie gave his broad back a speculative look. She didn't see how going to his aunt's house could take any longer than going to the store, but she didn't argue with his decision. She merely said, "That's great. And I think you should take Puppy with you."

He turned his head to stare at her. "Why would I do that?"

"Because he'd enjoy it. Besides," she added hastily before Luc could express his views on what the dog would enjoy, "he needs practice staying in the truck quietly at times. And it will be good for him to be exposed to a new environment, like a pet store. I know one that actually encourages people to bring in their pets."

Luc shook his head, but didn't protest any further. All he said was, "Fine. But if I have to take him, you're coming along."

And when the weekend rolled around, Luc dutifully put Puppy on his leash and led him over to the truck. He opened the passenger door and held it for Julie to climb in.

She regarded the high seat with disfavor. "Why is your truck so high? It's ridiculous to have those big wheels."

"Not when you're driving through deep mud on a job site, it isn't."

She grimaced at his answer, then her face brightened. "Let's take my Volkswagen!"

He gave her an incredulous look. "You're joking, right? There's a reason they call that thing a bug. I couldn't even get my legs in and as for Puppy…" They both looked at the dog sitting patiently by their side. "That's just not going to happen. Besides, I'd rather drive."

He stepped toward her impatiently. "If you'd just let me lift you in—"

"No!" She evaded his grasp, swatting at his hands when he persisted. "No, thank you," she said firmly. "I prefer to do it myself." She put her foot up on the floorboard. Luc moved closer, and she gave him a warning glance over her shoulder. "And don't help this time!"

He didn't. After she finally made it in, he told her to "Scoot over," then lifted Puppy up next to her.

"I keep meaning to do something about that," she said, sliding over a little to give the dog more room as Luc climbed into the driver's seat. "We need to teach him to jump in himself."

Luc grunted in response. It wasn't that he wanted to lift the dog in—the animal weighed a ton—but he was already devoting more time to the animal than he could afford. The only upside to the situation was that he was also spending time with Julie.

He glanced down at the top of her silky brown head as she shifted closer to his side in an effort to give the dog room. Luc didn't mind spending time with her at all. He got a kick out of her dry humor, and the sweetness of her rare smile made his blood surge. He hadn't dated any other women since she'd moved in; none appealed—none challenged him—the way Julie did. His growing attraction to her was an unexpected bonus to this setup. And before his time with Puppy was finished, he planned to get much, much closer to her.

He turned right, and she swayed with the movement of the truck, her slender shoulder bumping his arm companionably.

She immediately straightened in her seat. "Excuse me," she said politely.

"No problem." Luc frowned at the road. She sure was a cautious little thing, though. And so reserved. She used her manners like a shield, to keep him at bay. Still, those lazy hours in front of the television or fireplace were wearing her down—bit by bit. Every now and then, like when she'd come into the weight room, he'd catch a certain look in her eyes….

He shifted restlessly in his seat as he pictured that look, his body tightening. Oh, yeah, she wanted him all right. Lowering his eyelids to shield his gaze, he glanced down at her again and a slow smile curved his mouth. She just didn't know it yet.

Luc was still smiling as they entered the pet department store—or whatever they called the place. Stopping just inside the door, he gave a low whistle. "This place is huge."

On one side of the store were aquariums of all shapes and sizes. On the other were several rooms for pet grooming. In the middle were aisles and aisles of pet supplies. The strong, slightly sweet scent of cedar hung heavily in the air.

Luc gave Puppy, standing patiently at the end of the

leash, a doubtful look. "Are you sure they allow dogs in here?"

"Yes," Julie said confidently. "They even allow cats, if the owner wants to bring them in. And birds, too."

It sounded like the makings of a barnyard brawl, in Luc's opinion. Putting all kinds of animals together like that. But it wasn't his concern, so with Puppy on the leash, he paced down the aisles after Julie. He discouraged the mastiff from sniffing too vigorously at some hamsters trembling in their cages or pressing his nose against a large aquarium to go eye to bulging eye with a defiant blue-gray fish—species *Haplochromis burtoni*, according to the label on the glass. He shushed Puppy when he barked at a pertinacious purple parrot high on a perch.

But he couldn't shush the parrot. The bird apparently had pirate aspirations and kept demanding, "Hoist that sail, matey! Aargh, hoist it high, you landlubbers!"

Chuckling, Julie went on ahead when Luc and Puppy paused in front of what appeared to be a smorgasbord for dogs—a long counter filled with dog treats of every shape and kind. Luc was astounded by the selection. Beef biscuits. Chicken snacks. Even some that looked like chocolate chip cookies, guaranteed to "give your pet a whiter smile." They all actually looked good enough to eat.

Puppy apparently thought so. He snatched a cookie before Luc could stop him, swallowing it whole. Then sat there with an innocent look on his hairy brown face as Luc lectured him on stealing.

Since Puppy remained unrepentant, Luc decided it might be best to remove the hellhound from temptation and went hunting for Julie. They ran into her in the dog toy aisle.

She was standing in front of a bin filled with a variety of chew toys. Luc's brows drew down in a frown as he noticed what she was holding. "What's that?"

Julie glanced at the items in her arms. "A rawhide bone. A ball—"

"Not those," he said impatiently. "That baby blue thing in the cellophane."

"This?" She held it up so he could see it better. "It's an oversize pacifier made especially for dogs to chew on. Won't Puppy look cute with it?"

She held it out to Puppy, who sniffed it cautiously, wagging his stubby tail. Before he could take it, however, Luc removed it from Julie's grasp. "He's not going to walk around with a big, stupid pacifier in his mouth."

He tossed it back into the low bin, then checked over the selections quickly and pulled one out. "Here. *This* is the kind of toy a dog like Puppy should chew on."

Julie stared in horror at the plastic-wrapped toy he was holding up. "A fake cigar? You're not giving that to Puppy!"

Luc raised his eyebrows. "Why not? It'll be funny. He'll look like one of those poker-playing dogs in those pictures."

"It promotes smoking."

Luc rolled his eyes. "He's going to chew on it, for cripes' sake, Julie. Not puff on it."

"He's not going to have it at all," Julie declared. She reached into the bin to retrieve the pacifier. "This is what he should have. It even makes a noise."

She squeezed. The shrill squeal made Puppy flinch.

Luc grimaced. "Well, that's annoying." He squeezed the cigar, which emitted a flat, flubbery sound.

"And that's disgusting," Julie declared, wrinkling her nose.

"No, it's not. It's practical. You know how everyone always blames the dog when they pass wind. Now Puppy will have a ready-made alibi."

"Oh, stop. I'm getting him the pacifier. It's better for him." She read aloud from the label, "'Good for teeth and gums. Specially designed for large breeds such as Great Danes and *mastiffs.*'" She stressed the last word as if that clinched the matter. "Obviously, this is the one that Puppy would want."

"No, this one is." Luc looked at the wrapping on the giant cigar. "It says, 'Made especially for dogs that don't want to look like wimps.'"

"It does not!"

"Nope. You're right. It says, 'For dogs who can't read labels.' Hey, whadaya know! That's Puppy! I'm getting it."

He turned to leave, but Julie stepped in front of him, blocking his way. "Maybe we should let Puppy decide. He's the one who has to play with it, after all."

Luc considered the suggestion. "Okay. Sounds fair."

In the interests of impartiality, Luc insisted they return both toys to the low bin. Then he told Puppy, "Pick one out. Any one you want, it's yours."

It took a while for Puppy to get the idea. He seemed more interested in snuffling along the gray linoleum floor than in choosing a toy. But finally, in response to Julie's gentle urging, he lowered his head to nuzzle the toys in the bin—and lifted it out again with a giant orange carrot clamped in his muzzle.

Luc groaned. "He only grabbed that one because it's unwrapped. It probably has dog spit on it or something, and that's why he chose it."

"It doesn't matter. He chose it," Julie declared, disappointed but resigned. "We have to abide by his choice." But just in case Puppy had a change of heart, she discreetly picked up the pacifier, saying, "I need to grab a couple of items for the institute before we go."

She headed off down the aisle, but Luc lingered a moment to pull out the cigar and offer it to Puppy again.

Puppy, however, held on to his carrot.

"That's what comes of feeding you all those vegetables," Luc grumbled. "You're one confused animal."

He decided to keep the cigar in case the dog changed his mind. But it appeared doubtful. Puppy was pleased with his carrot. He pranced proudly along beside Luc as they hunted for Julie again looking, Luc told him, as if he were sticking out a bright orange tongue at everyone.

They finally found Julie again in an aisle featuring a wide variety of collars and leashes hanging on rows and rows of pegs. Other customers in the aisle moved aside as Luc and Puppy strolled up. A sharp-faced woman with a Scotch terrier on a leash led the dog discreetly off and the owner of a dachshund quickly followed. A young mother hurriedly shepherded her four children away, as well, when the runt of the litter—a miniature blonde in a stroller—exclaimed, "Doggy!" and extended a drooly, baby bottle, clearly inviting the mastiff to share a taste.

Julie didn't notice, but Luc was offended by the mass exodus. He might not be overly fond of the dog, but Puppy hadn't done anything to be so obviously shunned. Even if he was carrying a carrot in his mouth.

"Don't take it personally," Luc said to the mastiff as Puppy sadly watched the children leave. "I've gotten the exact same reaction at times."

Puppy looked up at him and faintly wagged his tail.

Satisfied, Luc dismissed the problem. He moved up behind Julie, to see what she was looking at now.

"Hey, look at this!" Reaching over her shoulder, he pointed at a red collar decorated with little brown reindeers stamped into the leather. Another nearby was decorated with white bunnies on green. "Holiday wear for dogs?" He shook his head in disbelief.

"Why not?" Julie replied. She eyed Luc beneath her lashes, stifling a smile at his disgusted expression. To pay him back a little for nixing Puppy's proposed pacifier, she reached out to finger a broad collar in a rose pink shade. Assuming a thoughtful frown, she said, "Wouldn't Puppy's brown coat look good with—"

"*No*. No pink." Luc wasn't budging on the issue. He studied her innocent expression suspiciously. "Why are you so determined to make him look like a wimp?"

"Believe me, Luc," Julie said dryly, glancing down at Puppy's big, muscular frame as he sat next to them, "nothing can make that dog look wimpy."

"Well, he's not wearing pink while I'm holding his leash." Luc elbowed her aside to examine the selection for himself, then lifted a broad, black spiked collar off the rack. "Now, this is more like it. *This* is the kind of leash a gladiator dog would wear. Either that, or someone with an S and M fetish." He dangled it in front of Julie's face, a wicked glint in his dark eyes. "Don't you think so?"

Julie suddenly became aware of an elderly woman peering at them over her glasses, and two teenage boys in black leather jackets who turned to listen avidly. "I wouldn't know," she said primly.

"Sure you do," Luc replied, ignoring her repressive tone. With a suggestive note in his deep voice, he added, "You're an *expert* on collars and leashes."

To Julie's annoyance, she could feel her cheeks heating up. In an attempt to discomfit him in return, she said sweetly, "No, I'm not. But why don't you try it on? I'd be glad to tighten it for you."

"Later, baby. Later." He gave her his wolfish smile, then howled with laughter as she fled away flushed with embarrassment.

Luc winked at the elderly woman, then he and Puppy went after Julie, still holding the spiked collar.

They caught up with her at the checkout desk. He paid for the Puppy's carrot without complaint, even insisting on paying for the pacifier he so heartily disapproved of when Julie laid it on the counter and the cigar he'd rescued from the bin, as well. Julie wrestled the spiked collar away to be put back on the rack, replacing it with one of supple brown leather. Dog vitamins and a huge bag of dry food were also added to Puppy's pile of supplies.

Julie paid for the items she'd gathered for the institute separately. Dog treats. Extra leashes. Training collars.

Luc frowned at the size of her bill. "You do make the people at the institute pay for that stuff when you give it to their animals, don't you?"

"Mmm," Julie replied noncommittally.

Luc eyed her in suspicion. "At least tell me you deduct them as a business expense."

"Of course," she replied loftily, making a mental note to do so in the future.

They headed back to the truck. When they reached it, Julie made Luc wait a minute before she climbed in. "I want to try something." Removing a dog cookie from her bag, she let Puppy sniff it. Then she placed it up on the high seat. "Get it, boy," she said.

Without hesitation, Puppy jumped in, gulped the cookie, then jumped back out again.

Sitting down on the pavement, he looked up at Julie expectantly.

Hands on his hips, Luc stared at the dog with narrowed eyes. "Well, I'll be— He's been playing me! All this time, making me lift him in."

Puppy tilted his head to the side, meeting Luc's gaze. Casually, he scratched himself behind one cropped ear.

"I'm sure he didn't do it on purpose, Luc."

But Julie failed to convince him—especially when Puppy refused to jump up into the truck again. Even the offer of a bribe no longer worked.

"He's not hungry anymore," she said, when Puppy ignored the treats she offered. But she was puzzled by the dog's behavior.

"Oh, he's hungry, all right," Luc declared grimly. "He's always hungry. He just knows he's annoying me."

"Of course he doesn't." But it certainly appeared that was what Puppy intended, Julie silently conceded. And, whether he meant to or not, the mastiff succeeded. Because in the end, Luc had to once again lift the dog into the truck so that they could leave.

Luc was still irritated as they made the trip back home. Julie made soothing noises now and again in response to his growling complaints about how the dog was taking advantage of his good nature, while turning the problem over in her mind.

His refusal to jump into the truck indicated that on some level Puppy was resisting Luc, that trust was still lacking in their relationship. But how to overcome the problem was something she wasn't quite sure how to do.

Chapter Six

The big question:

> To breed or not to breed? That is the question.
> *Finding a Studworthy Male,* Micky Thornspeare

The way to foster Puppy's trust in Luc occurred to Julie a few evenings later.

In accordance with the routine she'd established during the last month, all three were sitting in Luc's den after dinner and a walk. Even though the evening was mild, Luc had lit a fire. His gas fireplace was designed for aesthetic appeal rather than warmth. The jets were evenly spaced and shot out multicolored flames, providing a modernistic light show even when heat wasn't needed. Julie enjoyed watching the colored flames dance; she found the sight soothing. Puppy was watching them, too, his ears pricked forward in guard mode as they hissed and swayed.

Luc was staring at a baseball game on TV.

Julie wasn't that interested in baseball. Neither, apparently, was Puppy. Growing tired of guarding the fire, the big dog rose from his spot and gave himself a vigorous shake. Then he padded over to the end of the couch where Julie sat, pushing at her arm with his muzzle, hoping for a pet.

Julie ran her hand across the dog's broad skull, and scratched behind his cropped ears in just the manner she knew he liked best. Puppy half closed his eyes and a sound of pleasure—half sigh, half low moan—rumbled from his deep chest.

As close to a purr as a dog could get, Julie thought, smiling. She glanced over at Luc to see if he'd heard it, too, but he appeared absorbed in the game. Earlier, he'd changed out of the suit he'd worn to work into more comfortable clothes—torn jeans and a plain black T-shirt. Half-sprawled across the other side of the couch, he'd propped his big bare feet up on the coffee table as he stared at the television.

Julie scratched Puppy a little longer, then, with a final pat, stopped, not wanting to spoil the dog.

Puppy gave her a reproachful look, then wandered over to sit next to Luc. The mastiff never glanced at the man, but remained sitting—straight and tall—by Luc's side.

Luc didn't notice. He continued to stare at the television without moving. Something in the fixity of his gaze made Julie wonder if his attention was actually on the game at all. His heavy-lidded eyes were narrowed, his dark brows lowered in a slight frown of concentration. His lips were pressed into a firm line. He had a beer can in the hand resting on his thigh, but he hadn't taken a sip for the last ten minutes. She suspected his mind was on his work.

She became positive of it when the Yankee catcher dropped the ball, and the opposing team scored. The crowd went wild. The announcers exclaimed excitedly.

Luc didn't even blink.

"Catcher's doing a good job," she commented.

Still unmoving, Luc grunted in absent agreement.

Yes, he was thinking about work, all right, she decided. The phone had rung even more often than usual earlier, and for the last couple evenings, as well. Although Luc didn't discuss the specifics of his job with her, his increased preoccupation indicated some project was coming to a head.

Julie stirred reluctantly. Maybe she should excuse herself and let Luc get to work. But the room was so cozy and she wasn't tired yet. She stretched lazily. Besides, this was supposed to be Puppy's time. It didn't matter about Luc ignoring her, she thought, surveying his absorbed expression from beneath her lashes. Luc was under no obligation to entertain her—even if she *was* bored out of her skull by the silly game on the TV. But it didn't seem right for him to just ignore the dog. Especially since Puppy was reaching out to him—in his aloof, canine fashion—for the very first time that she could remember.

She frowned as it suddenly occurred to her that she'd never seen Luc pet Puppy—a necessary part of bonding. An essential ingredient, in fact, when it came to building an animal's trust.

It also occurred to her that Luc was tense—his long fingers were clenched around the beer can, and his wide shoulders appeared stiff. He definitely needed to relax a little, she decided. Paying attention to Puppy would help him do that. After all, study after study had proven that petting an animal helped a person relax, even lowered his blood pressure. Judging by Luc's preoccupied scowl, he could stand to have his blood pressure lowered.

So, what better time than now to accomplish both objectives? Get Luc to relax and help him bond with Puppy.

And give her something to do besides watch the baseball game.

"Luc," she said.

"Yeah?" he replied absently, obviously still deep in thought.

Julie sighed. "Luc," she said more firmly. "Why don't you pet Puppy?"

That got his attention. He glanced at her, raising his brows questioningly. "Why would I?"

"Because he needs affection."

His fingers flexed restlessly on the beer can. "C'mon…"

"Seriously, Luc. Touch is very, very important. A dog can sense your feelings through your touch. That's the way he learns to trust and bond with you."

Luc regarded Puppy doubtfully. Puppy returned his stare, appearing equally unconvinced. Luc glanced again at Julie. Tucked in the far corner of the leather couch with her feet curled beneath her, she looked relaxed and casual, clad in a soft yellow tank top and jeans, her dark hair loose around her shoulders. But he could tell by the look in her gray eyes that she wasn't about to *really* relax until he'd petted the pesky pooch.

With a sigh, Luc leaned towards Puppy. He gave the dog two brisk pats on the head. Then he leaned back, resuming his comfortably slouched position, his gaze returning to the game, his mind to the pros and cons of using several backers or relying on just one to finance the Costa Rica resort.

Puppy snorted and lay down, putting his head on his paws.

Julie snorted, too—although much more delicately. "You call that petting?"

"Yeah," Luc replied, without looking away from the television.

"Well, that was pitiful."

"I made an effort—"

"Oh, please," Julie interrupted, rising to her feet in exasperation. She stalked around the couch to stand next to him. "Which do you like better? This?" She gave Luc a couple of brisk taps on his head. "Or this?" She stroked his hair lingeringly, smoothing her fingers through the short, thick strands, caressing his scalp. Beguiled by the crisp, silky feel of his short hair, she did it again, unable to help herself.

Then she stopped abruptly.

Beneath her touch, Luc had stiffened, his senses leaping at the feel of her small fingers resting lightly on his hair. His mental calculations disappeared completely. All his attention shifted to focus on the woman standing still as a statue behind him.

He tilted his head back to look at her.

Julie appeared startled. Her lips were slightly parted, her eyes wide. Her pupils had flared, concealing all but the thinnest rim of gray on her irises as she met his gaze.

She blinked—then jerked her hand away to grip the back of the couch. "There," she said, huskily. She cleared her throat, but her voice still sounded odd as she added, "See what I mean?"

"Yeah," Luc drawled. He did see—much more than she meant to reveal. His gaze dropped from her averted gaze and flushed cheeks down to the base of her throat. A pulse beat rapidly in the delicate hollow. He glanced at her breasts. Her nipples were visibly erect, peaking against the soft, stretchy cotton of her tank top.

She intercepted his stare and crossed her arms over her chest. Her chin lifted. She said in a haughty tone, "Good. So now that you understand the difference…"

She started to move away. Luc reached up, snagging her wrist to hold her in place. "I want to try it again."

Her flush deepened. She tugged at his grasp, while looking down her small nose at him. "Oh, please. If you think I'm going to pet you again—"

"No, you've got it wrong." He pulled gently but inexorably until she was leaning slightly toward him over the arm of the couch. Reaching up, he grasped her shoulder with his other hand, saying, "I'm the one who's learning to pet, remember? I think I should practice on *you*."

And he tumbled her into his lap.

She sprawled across him. "Luc!"

Luc chuckled as she struggled to sit upright, jerking his chin back to avoid getting clipped by her head, then grunting as she jabbed him in his ribs with her sharp, pointed elbow. With an exasperated growl, he lifted her up, reseating her more comfortably. Wrapping his arms around her, he tilted her back over his forearm, cradling her in his hold.

He looked down into her face.

Her cheeks were dark pink, her smoky eyes flashing. "Luc, let me go—"

"No." He kissed the tip of her nose. He didn't want to let her go. She felt good in his arms. Warm and supple and delightfully wriggly. Maybe too wriggly, he decided when she started squirming around again. He tightened his hold to keep her in place.

"Stop it," he ordered and kissed her cheek.

"Me!" She lifted her head, almost clipping his chin again. Blowing her tangled hair out of her face, she glared at him indignantly. "*You* stop it. Let me get up."

"No way." Not when he had her right where he wanted her. He dropped a kiss on the corner of her frowning mouth.

"Luc…" she said in a warning tone.

He dropped a kiss on the other corner. He kissed her brow, then her vulnerable temple. He rubbed his cheek against the soft curve of hers, marveling at the satin smoothness of her skin

"Luc." This time her tone was more uncertain.

She'd stopped pushing him away and gone still in his arms. He trailed kisses along the vulnerable line of her jaw and felt her breath catch. Her fingers clutched his shirt. Her lashes tickled his cheek as her eyes fluttered shut.

"Luc," she said weakly, "stop it—"

His mouth closed over hers.

Her lips felt soft—swollen and tender under his. He lifted his mouth to brush his lips back and forth over the plump, sealed curves of hers, coaxing them to part. "Kiss me, Julie. Please, honey." With his mouth a fraction above hers he added huskily, "Open your mouth for me. You taste so sweet."

For a heart-stopping moment, she didn't move. Then, slowly, her arms slid up to encircle his neck. She clutched his nape. She drew his head down, her lips parting on a sigh.

Luc groaned low in his throat and his arms tightened around her. He kissed her deeply, his tongue sliding past her sweet lips to claim the warm softness beyond. She returned the caress, her tongue gently meeting his. His breathing roughened, his skin heated. His groin grew heavy with arousal.

Breaking the kiss, Luc buried his face in her hair. She smelled soapy sweet. Feminine. He speared his fingers into the silky mass, inhaling deeply. Cupping her head in his palm, he nuzzled her neck, stringing a line of tiny, nibbling kisses along the curve of her shoulder. His lips followed the delicate tendon in her neck, tracing it up to just beneath her ear where her pulse throbbed rapidly beneath his mouth.

He bit her gently.

She gave a tiny gasp, and her grasp on his shirt tightened. He laved her skin with his tongue, then sucked the spot, gently and then harder. Her fingers opened and closed, flexing in response to the drawing motion of his mouth.

His mouth traveled back to hers to kiss her deeply once again. Aching to have her closer, he grasped her hip to shift her on his lap, turning her so her breasts pressed against his chest. Her nipples stabbed at him, and he slid his hand beneath her top, stroking up along the smooth skin of her belly to cup her breast in his palm.

Her hand covered his, halting the movement. Her lashes fluttered up. Her eyes—he loved the soft, dazed look in her eyes. She looked vulnerable and sweet, desire warring with uncertainty in the gray depths. His arms tightened involuntarily, crushing her closer. Trapping her hand as it covered his between their bodies.

She lifted her other hand to his cheek. She stroked his skin, her fingers gently exploring the sandpaper texture of the whiskers along his cheek and jaw. Her gaze turned troubled as she searched his face. "Luc, I didn't mean to start all this—"

He pressed his lips against hers, stopping the words. "Yeah—yeah, you did," he murmured against her mouth.

Maybe she had, Julie thought, her eyes closing again as Luc kissed her. Maybe this is what she'd wanted all along. Because something inside her seemed to leap up at his touch. To rise on a tide of heat from deep in her womb as his hand skimmed over her stomach and back up to cup her breast. Her breast felt heavy, aching and aroused in his palm. His thumb circled her erect nipple, and she quivered, turning to bury her face against his neck.

"Luc," she moaned. His thumb brushed her nipple—
Rrrrrinnng!

The shrill ring of the phone pierced the sensual haze surrounding Julie. She tensed, wincing at the distracting noise. She started to pull away, but Luc's hold tightened, keeping her in place.

Rrrinnng!

His lips roved along her cheek to her mouth and moved gently against hers, urging her mouth to open again.

Rrrinnng!

Julie complied, and his tongue stroked hers, demanding a response.

Rrrinnng!

The ringing stopped. There was silence. Julie relaxed, her aroused excitement increasing as Luc slowly tugged up her shirt, revealing her bare stomach. Her bare breasts. From a distance she heard the machine click on, then Luc's deep growl echoed into the room. "Tagliano. Leave a message."

Julie pressed her breasts against his hard chest, rubbing against him. With an inarticulate murmur of satisfaction, Luc lowered his mouth to her nipple—

"Hello, darling," purred a sultry, feminine voice.

Julie stiffened, her eyes popping open.

The breathy voice continued, "I still want to go swimming with you, lover. In the nude…"

Julie shoved at Luc, struggling to pull down her top—to get off his lap.

"Please, darling. Give me a call. I'm so desperately lonely for you."

Finally freeing herself from Luc's arms, Julie scooted along the couch, out of his reach. Flushed and mortified, she sat up straight and brushed down her top, trying to smooth out some of the wrinkles. Quickly realizing the hopelessness of the task, she abandoned it, folded her hands together and fastened her unseeing gaze on the television.

With a sigh, Luc sat up, too, shifting to try to ease the aching tightness in his jeans. Leila couldn't have timed her call better if she'd planned it to cause him grief. He slanted a sidelong glance at Julie. She was sitting primly erect, hands gripped together in her lap, as far from him on the couch as she could get. Practically climbing up on the other arm, in fact. Her gaze was fixed on the weatherman dancing around the screen predicting sunshine for tomorrow. Big surprise for California. But Julie looked intent, absorbed by the report. Her hair was still charmingly mussed from their kissing, her cheeks pink, her lips slightly puffy. And her expression was as forbidding as a snowstorm in the Arctic.

"Julie…"

She didn't appear to hear him.

"Julie," he said a little louder.

She reluctantly glanced his way.

Luc coaxed, "Come closer, honey." He smiled. "Let's…talk a little."

She considered his smile for a moment, her eyes narrowing. Then she gave a decisive nod. A strand of her hair fell over her soft cheek at the movement and she pushed it back as she said, "You're right. There is something I've been meaning to discuss with you."

"Good." Luc didn't care what they discussed, as long as it got her mind off that phone message—and on to other, more important things. Like where they'd left off.

He slid a little closer to her along the sofa and put his feet back on the coffee table, trying to act casual, getting comfortable again. Reaching out to grasp her shoulders, he gently turned her to face him. His gaze dropped to her lips—swollen, red and just begging to be kissed again. With his eyes fixed on their ripe sweetness, he lowered his mouth towards hers, saying thickly, "What did you want to discuss?"

Her sweet lips moved. "Neutering."

Luc recoiled—releasing her as quickly as if she'd stabbed him with a knife. A sharp, surgical knife. "What!"

"We need to talk about neutering." Seeing his horrified expression, she added dryly, "Neutering Puppy, I mean."

"Yeah, I knew that." Of course he had. He ran his hand over his hair. The word had just triggered his—his protect-your-manhood-at-all-costs startle reflex for a second.

Luc frowned and sat up straighter. He lowered his feet to the ground, for some reason finding it impossible to remain lounging back during the topic under discussion. "But why would you want to neuter Puppy?"

"Well, for one thing, it might curb his tendency to roam."

"I'm sure it would curb a lot of things. But he hasn't run away lately and even if he had, isn't that a little drastic? Putting him under the knife?" The more he considered the idea, the more Luc didn't like it. His frown deepened. "Why, the idea is obscene—barbaric. And what about puppies?"

Julie lifted her brows. "What about them?"

"He might want puppies someday."

Surprise flickered across her face. "Do you want puppies?"

"Me? Hell, no!" The mere idea made Luc jump up from the couch. He paced away a few steps, then turned to pace back again. "Not now, anyway. Maybe not ever."

"Then the best option would be to neuter him."

"Would you quit saying that!"

"Not all dogs are studs, Luc."

"C'mon, Julie—the dog's Italian! Of course he's a stud. Hell, you yourself said he's a rare breed. It would be stupid to—" he winced involuntarily "—neuter a *Cane corso* mastiff in his prime. In any event, we are not neutering Puppy."

He crossed his arms, indicating the issue was settled. Puppy apparently considered it settled also. He rose to his feet. After a brisk shake, he trotted to the door.

Julie didn't argue any further. She simply regarded Luc for a moment, then shrugged and stood up. "Fine. If that's what you want—"

"It is."

"Then it's your decision. He's your dog, after all."

Yeah—lucky for Puppy, Luc thought. And now that that was settled…

He moved closer and ran his finger down Julie's arm. Her skin felt warm and smooth beneath his touch.

She stepped away.

He stepped closer. "Julie—"

"Woof!" Puppy's deep bark interrupted.

"I just want to tell you that woman—"

"Woof! Woof?"

"That woman who called means nothing to—"

"WOOF!"

"Damn it, Puppy! Quiet down! *Silenzio!*"

In the sudden calm, Puppy—and Julie—both looked at Luc with reproachful dignity.

"You don't need to yell, Luc," Julie said quietly. "He obviously wants to go out. I'll walk him to his crate."

Luc caught her hand, lacing his fingers through hers. "But I'm trying to tell you—"

She tugged her fingers free. "You don't need to tell me anything. I understand the situation completely." She walked to the door. "C'mon, Puppy."

The dog bounded out into the hallway, and Julie followed. "Good night, Luc."

"Wait a minute. I'll come with you."

Julie didn't argue; she strode briskly down the hall and out the back door, Puppy at her side and Luc beside Puppy. The hound remained between them as they crossed the lawn, and when they reached Julie's door, she turned the knob and opened it, still without speaking.

She reached out to give Puppy a good-night pat.

Luc propped his hand against the jamb, blocking her way with his arm as she turned to step inside. "Look, Julie…"

"Good night, Luc." She ducked neatly under his arm, then closed the door in his face.

Luc cursed beneath his breath. "Women!"

Puppy looked up at him.

"Yeah, I'm talking about her." Luc stared at the door. Resisting the urge to beat it with his fist, he turned away, saying irritably, "No use hanging around out here."

Luc started off toward Puppy's kennel, his gait stiff-legged with annoyance, the mastiff at his side. "She can be so touchy. I tried to tell her I wasn't interested in Leila—that that was over months ago—but would she listen? No."

They reached the dog's crate. Luc watched brood-ingly as Puppy went through his nightly ritual of sniff-ing around, then circling three times before lying down inside. "Not that you were much help," he added sourly. "Why did you keep interrupting like that?"

Finally settled, Puppy looked up at Luc and gave his usual sleepy, warning growl.

Luc frowned at him. "Yeah, well, I'm not liking you too much at the moment, either, so don't start. Instead of growling, you should be howling my praises, you in-grate. Believe me, if it wasn't for my timely intervention, you'd be barking in a much higher key from now on."

Puppy yawned and laid his head on his paws.

Luc turned and gave the guesthouse a long, consid-ering look. He'd try talking to her some more, he de-cided. Make her see reason.

He'd taken two steps towards her door when the lights clicked off.

Julie stood in the darkened guesthouse, listening to Luc's footsteps come closer to her door.

Her breath caught as they stopped outside.

The silence stretched. Then…slowly…he started walking again, his footsteps gradually fading into the distance.

Julie released the breath she'd been holding. She was trembling; she couldn't seem to stop. Moving clumsily, stumbling in the dark, she changed into her nightgown and climbed into bed.

She couldn't sleep. She tossed and turned, unable to relax. She got up to untangle her sheets, then lay down and twisted them up again.

The night's events kept replaying in her mind. She flushed hot with embarrassment, then shivered in reaction whenever she thought about the way Luc had kissed her, the way his warm hands had felt moving over her. How he'd cupped her breast, his thumb brushing her nipple. She rolled onto her stomach and buried her face in her pillow.

How could she have let that whole fiasco start?

She turned her head to the side, staring into the dark room. She wanted to blame Luc. It would be so much easier to blame him than herself. But he hadn't started that—that petting session on the couch. She had. All he'd done was to respond instinctively. Like any other normal, virile male.

She groaned and pulled her pillow over her face. No, it had been her fault, not his. She'd known better—on a logical level, at least. She'd recognized his appeal from the first day she'd moved in here, but she'd kidded herself into thinking she was immune to his raw charm.

Well, tonight had proven she wasn't.

She curled on her side—then rolled over again. A fine sheen of perspiration coated her skin as the memory of his lips moving along her throat filled her mind. He'd felt so hot, his touch had been so tender, so exciting. And his mouth. Her neck still throbbed with a heated pulse where his teeth had nipped her—

She sat bolt upright. She flicked on the light. She climbed out of bed, and stalked into the bathroom. Pushing her hair aside, she looked in the mirror at her neck.

A red mark marred her skin.

Appalled, she stared at the spot. Why that—that animal had marked her! He'd given her a love bite! A *hickey!* She hadn't had a hickey since—she'd never had a hickey!

With a groan, she headed back to her bed, flipped off the light, then flopped back onto the mattress to stare bleakly up at the darkened ceiling. She'd never had to deal with a man like Luc before. The men she'd dated in the past had all been pussycats compared to him— tame, predictable. Even a bit boring. She wasn't sure how to handle a man like Luc.

She wished she could talk to her mom; Jessica Jones had a practical way of looking at things that Julie had learned to value. Yet, although she loved her mother and knew her mother loved her, they'd never had the kind of relationship where Julie felt comfortable confiding something like this.

She'd lost touch with the friends she'd made in college. And although Georgia had become a good friend, she was also an employee. Julie wouldn't feel comfortable confiding in her either. Besides, why bother when Julie already knew what Georgia would say. "You'd have to be insane," she whispered fiercely in the dark. "To even think about getting romantically involved with that man."

And she wasn't insane. She was logical. Practical. A sedate, taxpaying citizen who owned her own business. She was reasonably intelligent; she could handle this unwelcome attraction on her own. All she had to do was get a grip. Leash in her desire. Take charge of the situation.

To begin with, she wouldn't hang around him so much, she thought grimly. Now that she had Luc and

Puppy established in a routine, she'd distance herself—from him and from Puppy. Give them a chance to bond even more. Maybe she'd work in the evenings. On her accounts. Or teach a class. Maybe she'd even go out on a date or two with someone else. Someone who wanted to settle down. Someone more her type.

Which Luc Tagliano definitely wasn't.

Luc Tagliano was stubborn. Bossy. A workaholic. A terrible, terrible tease. Worst of all, he'd been with who knew how many women. For goodness sake, the man was more of a roamer than Puppy!

She sat up to pound her pillow, then lay down again. She turned on her side and shut her eyes, determined not to even think about Luc again.

The man might be amusing. And shrewdly intelligent beneath his rough-hewn manner. And—*oh, admit it, you idiot!*—so sexy he could make her feel as if she were melting with nothing but a glance. But none of that mattered. He was undomesticated, wild and definitely dangerous.

Her hand crept up to her neck, pressing against the spot where her skin seemed to burn.

And she refused to get bitten again.

Chapter Seven

Territorial issues:

The canine community has a distinct social order. Heading this hierarchy is the pack leader, better known as the alpha dog. Usually the alpha dog achieves his status by being stronger or smarter than the rest.

Sometimes he's just more domineering.

As leader, the alpha expects first choice in everything, including a mate. Any other dog foolish enough to approach what the leader considers his will be quickly warned off with a direct stare and a low growl. If this is not heeded, the threats will increase to a snarl. He might raise a hind leg to urinate and then claw the ground like a charging bull, with his hackles raised.

When the alpha dog walks stiffly forward, his

gaze fixed on the transgressor, owners beware!
Attack is menacingly near.
The Top Dog, Ekul Ruane

Luc was late getting home the next evening.

The smell of frying beef and vegetables greeted him as he came in his front door. Shedding his coat and briefcase in the foyer, he headed toward the kitchen.

Julie was standing at the stove, her back to him, Puppy by her side. The dog glanced over at his entrance, but Julie's attention remained fixed on the food she was stirring in a pan.

Luc paused in the doorway. The sight of her working in his kitchen, preparing him a meal, gave him a strange feeling of satisfaction. All day long, thoughts of Julie had interfered with his concentration. He'd been anxious to see her, to settle their small misunderstanding from the previous night and to pursue this new direction their relationship had taken.

He propped his shoulder against the doorjamb and folded his arms over his chest, taking a moment to study her. She'd changed out of her work clothes into a swirly flowered skirt and a feminine blouse in soft pink. A silky white scarf was knotted loosely around her neck. Her slim waist was encircled by a crisp blue apron, the kind of bibbed apron he'd seen her use at the institute when demonstrating how to groom a dog. The bow of the garment hung right above her pert bottom, the ends trailing down to frame the sweet curves.

He eyed her sexy rear for an appreciative moment, then said softly, "Hi, there."

Her back stiffened. Then she glanced over her shoulder. "Hello."

Her voice was cool, her gray eyes equally so. Luc

lifted his brows as she immediately turned her back on him again.

He glanced at the dog. Puppy met his gaze blandly.

"Hey there, fella." Luc snapped his fingers lightly to coax the dog nearer. "How're you doing today?"

Puppy stared at him, then returned his attention to the pan.

"Not even going to come over and say hi?" Luc asked.

"He's hungry." Julie's tone was clipped. "He's accustomed to being fed by six."

"It's only eight. I'm not that late," Luc drawled. When she didn't reply, he added, "Besides, I thought you might feed him."

She swung around at that, the spoon upraised in her hand. Her apron had the institute's logo on the front, centered neatly over her breasts. "Oh? Why is that?" she asked. "Has our agreement changed for some reason?"

"No, but you've done it before. I didn't think you'd mind doing it again."

"I wouldn't have minded—if you'd called to ask me and if I'd been here. As it happens, I left work late, too. My car is broken again, and I had to have it towed to the shop."

"Oh. That's tough." He glanced at the dog again. "Well, waiting a couple hours to eat won't kill him."

Julie narrowed her eyes at him, then swung back around to stir the pan.

The savory smell wafting from the stove made Luc's stomach contract. He didn't owe her any excuses for being late, he decided. He wasn't on anyone's leash. Still, an explanation might mellow her mood. Hurry dinner along.

Yanking a chair away from the table, he spun it

around and straddled it. As he loosened his tie, he explained about the call that had come just as he had been walking out the door. He didn't mention it had concerned the Costa Rica deal—no sense going into useless details. But he stressed he'd needed to follow up on a few other things—very *important* things—as a result.

Julie glanced at him now and again, scrutinizing his expression as he talked, but she remained silent. She just listened—and listened—until damned if his perfectly reasonable explanation didn't begin to sound lame to his own ears.

Luc finished talking. And she still didn't speak. He pulled off his tie, and idly wrapped it around his fist as he waited. He'd grown up with Italian females—his mother and great-aunt—who hadn't hesitated to give him verbal hell whenever he had done something they hadn't liked. A lot of sound and fury and stomping around. Female tears and small fingers shaken in his face, amidst piteous gazes cast up at heaven and dire predictions of the disastrous future that awaited him if he didn't mend his ways.

Luc was used to that; he could handle it.

But Julie just kept stirring.

The silence lengthened; Luc's patience shortened. After a few minutes, he noted, with an edge in his voice, "Business has to take precedence over a dog's dinner schedule sometimes, Julie."

That got her attention. She whirled to meet his eyes in a level stare. "Of course it does, when it's absolutely necessary. But you're a successful businessman, right? In fact, *very* successful, judging by this house and your lifestyle," she added, with an expansive wave of her spoon.

"Yeah, so?"

"So isn't a measure of success having more free time? To be able to do what you want, when you want?"

"Well, yeah, but—"

"So the more successful you are, the more free time you should have, right?"

"In theory, yeah," he hedged. "But in reality, it's not that simple."

"So what you're saying is you're more tied to your work than someone who maybe doesn't earn as much but has more free time to spend on things they like to do."

"What I'm saying is that my business is complicated and I need to stay on top of things. I have business obligations to meet, major deals I give my word on."

He thought he had her. But then she said in a quiet tone. "You made a deal with me, too, Luc. And you have obligations to Puppy."

He shifted in his chair. "Yeah, well, that's different. I don't think being a little late a few times is that big an issue."

"Fine." She turned back to her pan. "Then there's nothing more to talk about." She flicked off the burner on the stove, the movement brisk and final.

Luc's jaw tightened. Easy for her to say. There was a lot more to talk about, in his opinion. But not about him being late or working so much or the dog having to wait for his dinner.

What *he* wanted to discuss was last night. Their kiss. Picking up where they left off.

Having sex.

He stared moodily at her pert bottom again. At the cute bow tied above it, and the rigid line of her spine

above the bow. It didn't take any special intuition to
know that *his* preferred topics of conversation weren't
going to be discussed anytime soon. At least not until
he'd settled this *new*, small misunderstanding that had
arisen.

"Okay, I'm sorry," he growled finally, breaking the
continuing silence. "I didn't intend for the dog to go
hungry." And he meant it. He didn't like to think of the
mastiff suffering. Being ravenously hungry himself at
the moment, he knew what that felt like. "And I didn't
intend to go back on my agreement. I shouldn't have
assumed you'd feed him. Next time, I'll make sure he's
taken care of somehow if I can't make it home."

Julie glanced at him, the tight press of her lips easing slightly. "Fine, then." Picking up the pan, she
walked away from the stove toward the countertop.

One thing settled, Luc thought. Now they could eat
in peace. He relaxed, setting his tie aside on the table—
only to stiffen in startled outrage when Julie suddenly
emptied the pan into Puppy's dish by the counter.

"Hey!" Luc protested. His stomach protested almost
as loudly, growling furiously as he watched Puppy dig
in. "Why did you do that?"

She straightened, pan in hand, her eyebrows arching
in surprise. "You wanted me to feed Puppy, so I did. I
thought he needed a few more fresh vegetables with his
meat, so I mixed up something special."

Disgruntled, Luc watched Puppy gulp down his
food, then he looked around the kitchen. The counters
were bare except for a bowl on the center of the table.
He reached into it and plucked out a brown cookie.

He was contemplating it when Julie said, "You do
realize that's one of Puppy's biscuits, don't you?"

"Yeah, I know." Luc was still tempted to eat it…but

finally tossed it back into the bowl with a disgusted murmur. Scowling, he rubbed his lean belly. "Isn't there any human food around here?"

Julie lifted her brows again. "I wouldn't know." She untied her apron and slipped it over her head. "This is your kitchen, remember. What did you do before Puppy and I moved in and I started cooking every night?"

"I didn't eat at home very often." He'd rarely even come home this early before Puppy and Julie had moved in. He'd work late, then stop off at some restaurant if any were still open, or hit a fast-food joint when they weren't. Part of the reason he was so hungry now was because he'd become accustomed to eating at a regular time every night, he decided. And that was Julie's fault.

"Let's go out," Luc suggested. "There's a nice little Italian place downtown that makes lasagna almost as good as Aunt Sophia used to. We can have wine. Relax…"

His voice trailed off. Puppy, looking up from his empty bowl, was watching him expectantly, but Julie was shaking her head.

"Thank you, but no. I already ate," she said, in a polite, definite, *distant* tone that made him want to shake her.

Luc stared at her a moment, watched her fold the apron into a precise little square. Then he rose and shoved his chair back under the table. "Fine," he said coolly and left the kitchen.

Julie stayed where she was. Her unseeing gaze fastened on Puppy's empty blue dish as she listened to Luc's footsteps head down the hall and into his office. Hearing Luc pick up the phone, she twisted the apron in her hands. *He's going to ask someone else,* she thought. Angry at the pang the thought caused, she tossed the apron aside and headed out of the room.

Luc glanced up sharply, phone in hand, as she strode past his open office door.

His brows lowered over his eyes. "Where are you going?"

"To work," she said abruptly.

Luc slammed down the phone to follow her. Puppy's toenails clicked on the marble tiles as he scrambled to follow Luc.

"What are you talking about?" Luc demanded, dogging Julie's heels as she headed down the hall to the front door. "You don't work nights."

"Tonight I am. Georgia has an especially promising pupil that she thinks merits some special attention." She paused in the foyer to remove her sweater off the coat rack.

"But it's late."

"Oh, please," she said dryly. "Not ten minutes ago, you told me it wasn't late at all."

Luc scowled, annoyed by her reasoning. "That's different. I was coming in. You're going out." Since that argument wasn't stopping her from sliding on her sweater, he pointed out, "Besides, how are you going to get there?"

Julie shrugged and picked up her purse. "I'm taking the bus."

"The hell you are," Luc said grimly. "Not at this time of night."

Julie froze, then turned to give him a "look." "I wasn't asking for your approval. So—" she turned toward the door "—if you'll excuse me—"

She reached for the knob to pull the door open.

Luc slammed a hand against the panels to stop her.

"Wait a minute. If you insist on going, I'll drive you. I might as well," he interrupted as she started to argue. "It would be stupid for you to wait around for a bus when I need to go out to get something to eat, anyway. I'll drop you off, grab a burger and pick you back up."

Refusal was still clear in her expression, so he added, "Riding with me will get you there sooner. Besides, Puppy wants to go. And it'll be good for him to get out after being stuck home all day."

Julie hesitated with her hand on the knob and looked down at Puppy. His whole hind end was wagging in delight.

Julie bit her lip. She fidgeted with the doorknob. "I'm not sure how long I'll be," she said, obviously weakening at the sight of Puppy's eagerness—just as Luc had known she would. "It might be an hour or two."

"No problem," he assured her. "Like you've said before, Puppy could use the practice of waiting quietly in the truck. It'll be good for him." Since she still looked torn, he added meaningfully, "And he sure looks excited at the prospect of going out."

The mastiff looked up at her, tongue lolling as he gave her a wide doggy grin before returning his expectant gaze to the door.

Julie hesitated a moment longer, then gave in. "All right, if you insist," she conceded grudgingly. "But I'm not rushing the lesson I'm giving," she warned Luc. "You might have to wait quite a while."

Luc shrugged as he plucked his keys and cell phone off the hall table and slipped his wallet into his back pocket. Fine with him. Besides eating, he had nothing planned for the evening anyway—except to get back into Julie's good graces.

And he certainly tried to do so on the way to the institute. He casually asked about her day; he commented on Puppy's progress. Julie responded with replies so brief as to be almost monosyllabic, her expression preoccupied.

Luc's frustration increased with each "yes," "no," "maybe," that she uttered. They reached the institute. Cars filled the small lot, but no one was around when Luc went to open the passenger door.

Puppy immediately jumped down. Without giving Julie time to argue, Luc put his hands on her waist and lifted her from the seat. He set her on her feet. Between his hands, her waist felt small and slim. It was stupid to be fighting like this, he decided. When they could be doing much better things.

His hands tightened as she began to pull away. He held her in place before him, determined to make her smile.

"Hey," he said softly, bending his knees to peer into her face, trying to catch her averted gaze. "Look at me a minute, will you?"

Her long lashes rose reluctantly. Her eyes met his.

"Let's not fight," he said coaxingly, pulling her closer. "After all, we're both adults here. And you know you're too mature to stay mad at me. And you're far too pretty for me to stay mad at you…"

A smile tugged at the corner of her mouth, and she hastily glanced away, biting her lip.

Encouraged, Luc added, "Especially tonight. You look so sexy in that skirt. And that scarf—" he gave it a playful tug, pulling it down farther on her slender throat. "It makes me want to—hey, what's this?" He drew his head back to see better. He pulled the scarf down more, then gently brushed his thumb over the mark on her slim white neck. "Ah, ha," he said, as understanding dawned. "So that's why you're wearing a scarf."

Her hand flew up to cover the bruise, and her gaze flew up to meet his. Even in the dusky light, Luc could see her cheeks redden.

He smiled, feeling a sense of primitive satisfaction. Personally, he thought the mark looked kind of sexy. A small reminder of the passion—albeit unfulfilled—that they'd shared. Indulgently amused by her embarrassment, he dropped a kiss on her nose. "Don't worry, honey. It's no big deal."

Her eyes narrowed. Luc could almost see icicles form in the gray depths as she said coldly, "Not to you maybe!"

She shoved at his chest, and he released her. She stalked past him, heading toward the training grounds.

Luc watched her go. Then shaking his head, he glanced down at Puppy, who was also watching Julie's retreat. "Women."

Puppy responded with a gruff bark, and an allover shake.

"Gave you the chills, did she? I'm not surprised. Talk about blowing hot and cold." Shaking his head again at the perversity of women—and one specific woman in particular—Luc lifted Puppy back into the truck, then headed to the nearest drive-through restaurant.

Two chili dogs and a cheeseburger later, Luc was still discussing Julie with Puppy as they sat in Luc's truck in the restaurant's parking lot.

"What's with that woman?" he asked the mastiff. "She's sure got her tail in a twist over last night. I can't understand why she's so upset over a small mark on her neck. If you ask me, she needs to loosen up. To quit being so uptight all the time. This is a whole new millennium, for crissakes. It's time for her come out of the dark ages and live a little."

He reached into the bag and pulled out another cheeseburger. "Yeah, she's way too uptight—that's her problem. And talk about a control freak. She worries about everything. Take you, for instance." He gestured with his burger at Puppy, who followed the movement intently. "You know—and I know—that a few burgers aren't going to hurt you. But does Julie the Doggy Dietitian agree? Oh, no. All she cares about is giving you vegetables."

He took a bite of his burger and glanced at the dog. "Don't give me that sad, deprived, big-eyed look," he warned the mastiff. "It might work on her, but I'm no sucker. I saw that meal she gave you. And we both know she'd skin my hide if I gave you fast food."

Puppy's brown eyes grew sadder. His head sank a little.

"Well…" Luc lifted the top off his bun. "…I guess a pickle won't hurt you. It's a vegetable, right? Want to try one?"

Puppy did.

Luc tossed it to him, and Puppy gulped it down.

So Luc gave him a tomato. "This is a fruit, not a vegetable," he warned the mastiff.

Puppy didn't care; he liked that, too. He also liked the onions and lettuce. And the cheese. And the meat.

Luc regarded the empty bun consideringly. "You aren't on a low-carb diet, are you?"

Puppy wasn't. The bun disappeared in one giant gulp.

Luc crumpled up the wrappings and stuffed them

back in the bag. He glanced at his watch. Now that he was no longer hungry and could think a little more clearly, he was anxious to talk to Julie again. Determined to straighten her out about her uptight, misguided attitude. "We may as well head back to the institute," he decided. "I can make some business calls while we wait. You ready to go?"

Puppy was. He crowded closer to Luc, trying to muscle his way into the driver's seat. But Luc shouldered him back onto the passenger's side, saying firmly, "I'll drive. You ride shotgun. Hopefully by the time we get there, she'll be ready to go home."

When they returned to the Institute, however, the parking lot was still full of cars. Luc cruised slowly past a restored '64 Corvette, idling his engine as he admired the black car's classic lines. Then he drove on toward the trees clustered at the other end of the lot. He parked, facing the training grounds so they could see the class still in session, illuminated by the hard, golden glow cast by the massive stadium lights.

Since the cab felt stuffy with Puppy panting out huge gusts of burger breath—the onions had been a mistake—Luc rolled down the windows. Ms. Irenmadden's barked commands drifted toward them on the light evening breeze. Even from a distance, her sturdy figure and iron-gray hair were unmistakable as she stood watching the owners march their dogs past her on the wide circular track—all heeling, trotting, running—in regimented response to her commands.

"Where's Julie?" Luc asked Puppy, frowning as he scanned the scene through the windshield. "I don't see—ah, there she is."

Julie was standing off to one side of the class, near the obstacle course. The white scarf was still tied around her neck. The fluttering ends of the material danced with her tousled hair in the breeze. She absently brushed it back as she talked to a tall guy with curly black hair who was holding the leash of a large black poodle. The biggest poodle Luc had ever seen. The dog's hair was sculpted in a fancy design, with a large pouf on the top of his head and a matching pouf at the end of his long, skinny tail.

Puppy leaned forward, ears cocked, to stare intently through the windshield at the poodle.

Luc elbowed the mastiff in the ribs. "I guess that's the promising pupil, huh? What do you think of his haircut?"

His gaze fixed, Puppy shifted slightly and gave a low growl.

"Yeah, that's my opinion, too. But each to his own, right? He's probably a French poodle. I imagine they go for that designer style."

Luc gave Puppy a careless pat, then reached into his pocket for his phone. He slouched back, stretching his legs to the side and resting an arm on the wheel to get comfortable. "Now, be patient," he admonished the mastiff, snapping his cell open to make the business call he'd started to put through earlier at the house. He glanced towards the obstacle course again. "Julie'll be done in a minute and—"

He broke off. Poodle Guy had moved closer to Julie, and he suddenly lifted his hand to run his fingers through her hair next to her cheek.

Luc jerked upright in angry amazement. "What the hell?"

Puppy gave an excited woof, but Luc ignored him. He kept watching Julie, waiting for her to slap the guy or something. She didn't. She didn't even move away.

She remained still, looking up into the guy's face, and damned if Poodle Guy didn't do it again, threading his fingers right through her hair.

She did move away then, shaking her head lightly and combing her own fingers through the tousled strands. Then she started walking toward the cones marking the start of the course.

And there was Poodle Guy, prancing along right beside her—even steadying her with a hand on her arm when the poodle bumped her and she stumbled a little.

Julie laughed. Poodle Guy laughed.

Luc growled, low in his throat.

Closing his cell phone with a snap, Luc slid it into his pocket. He narrowed his eyes to study the other man with militant interest. Poodle Guy was tall and athletic-looking in jeans and a long-sleeved blue T-shirt, and—from what Luc could tell from this distance—appeared to be about Luc's own age. He also appeared to be having way too much fun for a simple dog-training lesson. He and Julie were laughing together again as the poodle cavorted around them. Then they fell into an earnest conversation once more, Poodle Guy's dark, curly-haired head bent over Julie's silky brown one as he listened to what she was saying.

"What is she doing?" Luc demanded of Puppy. "This is the twenty-first century. There's all kind of kooks around. Doesn't she have enough sense to keep her distance from guys like that? She's way too friendly for her own good."

And Luc didn't like it.

"C'mon," he said to Puppy, picking up his leash. "Let's get over there. I don't trust that Poodle Guy."

Puppy scrambled out of the truck after him. Puppy didn't trust the poodle.

Absorbed in watching her client direct his dog through the obstacle course, Julie didn't notice the approaching pair at first. She was so intent on evaluating the owner's use of hand signals to guide the black standard, that when Georgia tapped on her shoulder, she gave a small start.

"What's up?" Julie asked, mystified by the trainer's concerned expression.

"Trouble's heading this way," Georgia said in an undertone, nodding her head in the direction of the parking lot. "You might want to go out and intercept them."

Alarmed by her friend's warning, Julie glanced over to where Luc and Puppy were approaching across the field. Rapidly, she assessed the animal with experienced eyes. Puppy was straining at the leash, his gaze fixed on the poodle. He wasn't snarling, but Julie realized immediately why Georgia was concerned. His cropped ears were laid back and his gait stiff-legged. "Puppy does look a little hostile," she conceded. "But Luc has him on a leash—"

"Yeah, but who's going to leash Tagliano?"

"What?" Julie's astonished gaze shifted from the dog to the man. They were still about thirty yards away, but even from that distance, Luc's hard, set expression was unmistakable in the bright overhead lights. His rapid stride was stiff with irritation. *What's his problem?* she wondered. "He's probably gotten tired of waiting," she speculated aloud. "I knew he'd get bored just sitting in the truck."

"Uh-huh. That's probably it," Georgia said dryly. "At any rate, you'd better go talk to him, because he's definitely ticked off about something."

Georgia was right, Julie decided as the trainer returned to her class. Even the rigid set of his shoulders attested to Luc's volatile mood. After calling out to her client that she'd be right back, Julie headed toward Luc and Puppy.

Luc stopped when she reached his side, but his gaze remained fixed on the man waiting by the obstacle course. Hands on his hips, Luc demanded, "Are you ready to go?"

"No."

That brought his gaze to her face. His brown eyes narrowed as he looked down at her, and a muscle flexed in his lean cheek. "No? What's taking so long?"

Julie folded her arms across her chest. Just as she'd suspected, he'd gotten tired of waiting. "My lesson with Sparky isn't finished yet."

Luc snorted, his narrowed gaze shooting back to her client. "Sparky? He named his poor poodle Sparky?"

Julie spoke slowly and distinctly. "The dog's name is Dynamite. The client's name is Sparky—Willard Sparklan Jr. to be exact. You may have heard of him," she added, as recognition flickered across Luc's face. "His father, Willard Sparklan Sr., was just elected to the state senate."

"Yeah, I've heard of the family, but not this guy," Luc drawled. He shook his head pityingly. "With a name like Willard Junior, it's no wonder he goes by Sparky. Can you keep a straight face when you say it?"

"Yes, I—oh, never mind about Sparky. Is there a reason for this interruption?"

"Yeah, Puppy is ready to go. So if you can persuade Junior to finish it up and quit wasting time stroking your hair—"

"Oh, for goodness sake, he wasn't stroking my hair!" Julie said, her cheeks heating with embarrassed annoyance. "He was helping untangle a ladybug that had gotten caught."

"Oh, yeah?" Luc stared across the field at the other man a moment longer, then dismissed him with a shrug. He looked down at Julie again. "Whatever. Let's go."

He turned, preparing to head back to the truck, but Julie didn't budge.

"I'm not done here yet," she said firmly. "I'm teaching Sparky how to direct Dynamite using hand signs, and he's still confused on a few." She glanced down at the mastiff, who was still watching the poodle intently. "But if Puppy can't wait—"

"He can't."

"Then I'm sure I can find someone else to give me a ride home."

Luc clenched his teeth. Yeah, he was sure she could find someone else, too. Without a doubt Sparky Junior would jump at the chance—and probably do a couple of somersaults for good measure. "We'll wait," he said abruptly. He took a step forward. "We'll just watch a while—"

Puppy suddenly lunged forward, barking ferociously his eyes fixed on the poodle.

Luc held on to the leash, but it wasn't easy. Biceps bulging and feet planted in the grass, he cursed beneath his breath as Puppy yanked him forward a step. "Damn it—"

"Puppy! Sit!" Julie ordered.

Puppy stopped lunging, but gave a low growl, shifting restlessly with his gaze still on the other dog.

"Sit! *Silenzio!*" Luc ordered.

Puppy slowly sat, whining in earnest protest.

Julie glanced back at the obstacle course. The poodle was standing still, his stance alert, his head turned in their direction. The dogs in Georgia's class were shifting restlessly, as well.

"Get Puppy out of here please," she told Luc. "Right now. He's distracting Dynamite."

Puppy growled and stood up again, his gaze fixed on the poodle staring at them from the obstacle course. Luc glanced over. Sparky was watching them, too. Luc's jaw tightened, but he gave a tight nod. "Fine. We'll meet you at the truck."

Julie didn't reply but immediately turned to head back to her client, posture regally erect, her hips swaying gently. And the ends of that damned scarf fluttering in the breeze. Luc stared after her a moment, then with a disgusted sound, turned to stalk back to the parking lot, pulling Puppy along with him.

Puppy stalked by his side, whining and growling in protest.

"Can it," Luc advised him.

Puppy quieted, and walked a little faster.

Luc glanced back over his shoulder. Julie was talking to Poodle Guy again, making broad sweeping gestures with her arm. "I know a hand sign I could show good old Sparky," Luc muttered to the mastiff, "and I'll bet he'll know exactly what it means."

Puppy woofed in agreement.

When they reached the truck, Luc lifted Puppy in, then climbed in beside him. They sat in brooding silence. Ms. Irenmadden's class ended, and the students and their pets wandered toward the parking lot. They climbed into their cars and gradually dispersed. Ms. Irenmadden left as well, acknowledging the truck's inmates with a sniff and reluctant nod as she passed.

Julie, the poodle and Poodle Guy kept working.

Luc growled in disgust, shifting restlessly. He folded his arms, and frowning, sank further in his seat. What the hell was taking so long? He'd just decided to leave

Puppy in the car and go over there again when the grounds' stadium lights went off. Only the light illuminating the parking lot and smaller lights around the building remained lit.

Julie must have them all set on a timer, Luc decided. Not a bad way to signal that a lesson was definitely over.

Sure enough, the three began walking toward the parking lot—more slowly than Luc thought was necessary—with Sparky crowding close on one side of Julie, the poodle on the other.

"Finally," Luc muttered between his teeth. Puppy whined and stiffened as the poodle drew nearer.

But instead of coming straight to the truck, Sparky Junior led Julie over to the 'Vette Luc had admired earlier. Sparky opened the back door and put his poodle inside, and closed it again. Then he leaned back against the window, idly slapping the leash he held against his palm as he continued talking to Julie.

Gritting his teeth, Luc waited. One minute. Two minutes. By the time three minutes had passed, he'd had enough. "That's it," he told Puppy.

He climbed out of the truck, and Puppy scrambled down after him before he could shut the door. Grabbing Puppy's leash, Luc started walking toward the Corvette.

Across the lot, Julie heard the truck door slam. She sensed Luc approaching, but forced herself to keep her attention on Sparky.

"This has been very beneficial, Julie," Sparky was saying. "I think Dynamite will catch on in no time, if I can keep everything straight." His pleasantly even features crinkled in a rueful grin, and he ran his hand through his curly hair. "Sorry to keep you here so late. I can't believe I kept messing up so much."

"You did fine," Julie said reassuringly. "All it takes is a little—"

Her nape tingled. She lifted her hand to rub the back of her neck through her scarf and smiled brightly at Sparky. "Well, I'd better get going. My ride's waiting. If you need any more help before Dynamite's first competition, just let me know."

"Actually..." Sparky straightened away from his car and stepped closer, touching her arm as she was about to turn away. "I still have a lot of questions right now." He glanced over her shoulder, then leaned closer. His voice dropped to a low, intimate tone. "How 'bout you tell your ride to go on home and we'll continue our discussion at my house over a cup of coffee. Or better yet, a glass of wine."

Julie blinked, surprised by Sparky's offer. She wondered if Luc, who had come up beside her, had heard it, too.

Unsure how to reply to Sparky, she stalled by introducing the two men. "Sparky, this is Luc Tagliano. Luc, Willard Sparklan."

"Tagliano," said Sparky.

Luc nodded briefly. The two men stared at each other, the overhead light cutting through the darkness to soften Sparky's handsome face, while casting the hard planes and angles of Luc's rough-hewn features into harsh relief.

Luc shifted closer to Julie, his arm brushing hers.

Sparky glanced at their arms, and his dark brows lifted questioningly as he said to Luc, "You're Julie's—?"

"He's my landlord. Temporarily," Julie interjected, before Luc could reply. "He was going out, so he offered me a ride tonight."

"Yeah," Luc shifted closer to her, a solid shadow at her back. "Julie's staying at my place."

Trust Luc to phrase it that way! Julie thought, her lips tightening. "I'm helping him," she said distinctly. "To train Puppy."

"Oh. Yeah." Luc gave her a blank look. "Yeah. Right."

Julie glared at him. He smiled. At least, Julie supposed it was meant to be a smile. A lot of sharp, white teeth were certainly on display.

Sparky glanced uncertainly from one to the other and then at Puppy, whose attention was fixed on the poodle framed in the car's back window.

The poodle growled. The mastiff growled louder in return. Sparky frowned at him. "Puppy? That's an unusual name."

"Yeah, it sure is, *Sparky*," Luc drawled. "We call him that because he's not fully grown yet."

"Oh, I see." Sparky ran his gaze over the mastiff, then said with a knowledgeable air, "Pit bull mix, hmm?"

"No. Italian."

Sparky frowned again at the dog's unwavering surveillance of the poodle. "He looks dangerous. Is he aggressive?"

"When he needs to be," Luc said softly.

Sparky's expression tightened at his tone. Seeing his reaction, Luc casually reached up to wrap a hand around the back of Julie's neck.

He rested his palm on her delicate nape, right over her silk scarf. Beneath his hold, he felt Julie stiffen. Yeah, she knew he was staking a silent claim on her. And *he* knew she didn't like it.

Well, tough.

Because there was no way he'd let her go out with Junior here.

He kept his gaze leveled on the other man. "If you'll excuse us, Sparky, Julie's ready to go home. I'm ready to go home. And most important, Puppy's ready to go home. Isn't that true, Julie?"

He glanced down and met her eyes. She was angry all right. He wondered if she'd argue; he didn't think so. Julie would hate making a scene, and she'd know it wouldn't bother him in the least.

But then he saw her chin come up.

She turned to Sparky. "I—"

"WOOF!"

Puppy charged the poodle. The black dog met him headfirst at the glass.

Snarling and barking furiously, they went muzzle to muzzle scratching and biting at the glass, barking and growling savagely. Dynamite dug determinedly at the upholstered interior and gnawed at the door handle to get to the mastiff. Puppy raked his claws down the car's gleaming finish and banged his broad muzzle and teeth against the window, trying to bite his way through.

The melee was deafening.

"Hey!" Sparky shouted frantically, trying to be heard above the animals. "Call off your dog!"

"Puppy! Sit!" Julie said sharply. "Silence!"

Surprised by the unaccustomed severity in her tone, Puppy promptly obeyed, but remained on alert. His big body quivering with tension, Puppy stared at Dynamite who—convinced he'd won the battle—started yapping and dancing triumphantly along the seat.

"In your dreams, Frenchie," Luc told him, then glanced at Dynamite's owner.

Like his dog, Sparky was yapping, too, making yelping noises as he ran his hand over the scratches imbedded in the Corvette's rich finish.

"Look what your mutt did to my car!" he said. Fists clenched around the leash, Sparky swung around to glare at Puppy—who was raising his hind leg over the Corvette's rear bumper.

Sparky's pleasant features twisted into a mask of anger. He raised the leash he was still holding, brandishing it like a whip as he said, "Why, you ugly, lowbred brute. I ought to—"

"Mr. Sparklan!"

Luc, who had taken a step toward the dog, prudently stayed still, holding Puppy back as Julie stepped in front of them to confront the other man.

"Puppy didn't harm your car on purpose!"

Sparky tried to speak, to argue his side, but Julie cut through his explanation. "There's no excuse for threatening a helpless animal in the way you did—"

"But—"

"I suggest you take Dynamite home," Julie concluded. "And I also suggest you find another training facility. Good evening."

She turned on her heel to march toward the truck. Luc and Puppy fell into step behind her.

Before they reached the vehicle, Sparky had slammed into his car. Two seconds later, he revved his engine and peeled out, tires squealing.

Luc and Puppy turned to watch him go. Then Luc looked down at Puppy, and Puppy looked up at Luc.

Luc gave a chuckle. "Good boy! Good, good boy!" he said, still chuckling as he rubbed Puppy's head enthusiastically. "Way to go, Puppy!"

Puppy bounced on his front paws, happy with the praise, panting excitedly.

"It's not funny."

Julie's cold tone stopped Luc in mid-laugh. Puppy quit bouncing.

Julie waited in silence for Luc to unlock the door so she could climb in. Luc lifted Puppy in after her, then went around to climb in himself. He settled in his seat and glanced at her frozen profile. "C'mon, Julie. You have to admit, the guy was a jerk."

"Please," Julie's icy tone sliced through the warm evening air. "If you want to talk about jerks, Luc Tagliano, then I suggest you start with your own behavior."

"Now, Julie—"

"Don't talk to me. You weren't only rude, but crass."

Luc shook his head sadly, as he turned on the ignition. "C'mon, Julie, don't be like that."

Her stiff, disapproving expression didn't change.

Luc sighed. Letting the engine idle, he rested his forearm on the wheel as he turned to face her. "Look, I'm sorry that Puppy piss—marked—Sparky's tires. But when you go by the name of Sparky, hell—you're almost begging to get hosed."

That did it. The remark about Sparky really lit her fuse. For the entire drive home, Julie lectured Luc without stopping, barely pausing to draw a breath. She told him exactly what she thought of his manners and his morals and even touched on the topic of his poor eating habits. She tore apart his character and gave a ten-minute dissertation on his misguided sense of humor alone.

But what really kept her going was his "audacity, arrogance, the sheer nerve" he had to think he could tell *her* what to do. Who did he think he was? she demanded, in a dangerously quiet tone that made Luc wince and Puppy whimper, to interfere in her personal business? Who was *he* to decide whom she could and could not date? What, she wanted to know, did he have to say for himself?

Nothing, she answered the question for him. Because he had the social sensitivity of a rock.

She was still exploring that topic when they parked at the house. Luc let Puppy out—and then made a misguided attempt to help Julie. She slapped his hands away and jumped down by herself. Then she crowded up against his chest to shake a slender finger in his face, while she predicted the sorrowful, horrible and hopefully terribly painful demise that awaited him if he didn't learn to mind his own business.

"And don't give me that hurt, poor me, wounded look!" Julie warned him, in a fuming tone as they stood by the truck. She clenched her fists by her sides, trying to resist the urge to punch him as he stood with his arms crossed, listening to her without saying a word. "You're nothing but a troublemaker, Luc Tagliano," she told him bitterly. "You have no excuse for behaving in such a rude and overbearing manner."

"Yeah, I do."

"Oh?" She pounced on that. "What is it?"

"I want you."

Julie sucked in a breath. The night seemed to swirl around her, then grow still. She slowly released the breath she was holding and stared up at him in the dark.

His face was half shadowed, half illuminated by the front porch light. He had a slight smile on his lips, but his gleaming eyes were disconcertingly intent.

Her heart skipped a beat. Her nape tingled in alarm. Suddenly aware of how close she stood next to him, she swallowed and backed up a step.

Then, rallying her defenses, she lifted up her chin.

"And you think *that* gives you the right to interfere in my personal life?"

"Yeah." His smile turned wolfish. "Because you want me, too."

Chapter Eight

Correcting problem behavior:

Some pets think they own you, rather than the other way around. If your pet believes he's in charge, then it's time for a major alpha attitude adjustment. In the canine world, the alpha dog receives a lot of attention from his followers in the forms of grooming and touching, which are indications of submission and respect. The alpha is usually the most vocal in a pack, as well.

So, to improve your animal's attitude, totally disregard any howling or whining. Pretend you don't hear a thing. Cut down on the amount of petting he receives, also. Don't let him paw or rub against you. If he keeps bothering you, tell him "No!" and ignore him. Until he learns his lesson,

only give him affection when *you* decide the time
is right.
De-Alpha-Petizing, Joel McCauley

At midnight, a scotch and water in hand, Luc lounged
on the couch in his darkened den, pondering the evening, trying to figure out where he'd gone wrong.

He stared into the darkness unseeingly. Clear in his
mind was the image of Julie's face when he'd stated that
she wanted him. The moment when—for the briefest
instant—the truth had flashed in her eyes.

He took a swallow of his scotch. Yeah, she wanted
him all right. He wasn't mistaken about that.

No, his mistake had been in stating it so bluntly. Because then she'd had a chance to deny it. And with a
resolute, if shaky, "No, I don't," she'd done so, then escaped to the guesthouse.

He'd let her go, of course. Just for the time being.
He figured she was upset by the whole Sparky episode.
That she needed space to calm down and realize what
she and Luc had going between them. The whole thing
had obviously taken her by surprise.

Hell, he'd been surprised, too. He took another drink.
He'd known he wanted her. But he hadn't realized how
much he wanted her until Sparky and his poodle pranced
onto the scene. He'd certainly never gotten jealous before.

Then again, he'd never known a woman like Julie before. She was different from the others. He'd realized
that from the first day he'd met her. Instead of coming
on to him, making an effort to please him, she'd lured
him on, day by day by…well, by simply being Julie.

She gave the dog as much attention—*more*—than she
gave him. And she rarely got dressed up, which just

made him speculate all the harder about what her trim little body—her breasts, her stomach, her sexy little bottom—looked like beneath her modest, practical outfits.

Yeah, she was laying down lures, all right, he decided, swirling the remaining liquid in his glass. She just didn't know it. But if she hadn't intended to catch his interest, she shouldn't have been so sweet and smart, so funny and downright sexy in her own prim, restrained way. She certainly shouldn't have moved into his guesthouse. The women he'd dated before had stayed on the edges, outside of what he considered his real life of home and work. But for over a month now, he'd seen and talked to Julie every day. He'd begun to look forward to spending time with her when he came home in the evenings. And, although the possessiveness he felt towards her was unexpected, it went bone deep. Far beyond uncertainty. Which made sense, when he thought about it. After all, he'd found her. He'd brought her home. She belonged to him now.

All she needed to do was admit it.

He set down his glass. The problem with that conclusion was it appeared she wasn't going to admit it—not right away, anyway. And he didn't have time to fool around, to give her the space to make the realization in her own sweet time. The Costa Rica deal was coming to head. If he wanted to proceed with the resort project, he needed to get down there to make some decisions.

Before he left, he wanted this whole Julie problem resolved, wrapped up, and Julie in his bed. He wanted to make sure she'd be waiting for him when he got back. To accomplish that quickly, he obviously needed to change tactics.

He needed to go on the hunt.

Leaning back, he linked his hands behind his head as he explored that solution. He wasn't experienced at chasing women; he'd never had to be. They'd always chased after him, rather than the other way around.

Luc smiled in the dark. But luckily, he'd had tutoring recently from an expert in the bonding process. All he needed to do was use all the good advice Julie had been giving him—

On Julie.

Luc initiated his plan the next day. He called the Puppy Institute from work.

"I have a favor to ask you," he said when Julie came on the line.

"Yes?" Her voice sounded cautious.

He kept his own tone brisk and impersonal. "I have a lot of work to do here—I may be late again. I don't want Puppy to have to wait for his dinner two nights in a row, so I was wondering if you'd mind feeding him again tonight?"

"Sure," she agreed readily, a hint of relief in her tone. "No problem."

"Thanks."

Luc set down the phone, smiling as he leaned back in his chair. No, it had been no problem at all to make sure she came home on time.

And he did the same. He arrived home at six and saw her Volkswagen parked in the driveway.

He parked behind her and strolled into the house. He caught her in the kitchen. Still in her work clothes, she was crouching by the cupboard, putting away Puppy's food. She straightened when she saw him, her eyes widening then narrowing in suspicion.

Puppy didn't even bother to look up from his dish.

"I got off on time after all," Luc said easily. He held out the treats he'd brought—candy and flowers—offering them to her with his best no-big-deal expression and an apology. "I'm sorry for the way I acted last night. Do you think we can just forget about it?"

He could tell by her expression that if she could have found a polite way to do it, she would have refused his request and his peace offerings. So he added with just a hint of a challenge in his voice, "After all, if you don't want me like you said, then what's the big deal?"

"It's not a big deal," she answered swiftly.

"Great. Thank goodness that's settled," Luc declared. "All day, I've been worrying about the effect our arguing might have on Puppy."

Julie glanced at Puppy, who was briskly pushing his empty dish around the marble kitchen floor with his nose. "We really shouldn't fight," she agreed dryly. "For Puppy's sake."

So—for Puppy's sake—she accepted the candy and bouquet of sweet-smelling roses. While she put the flowers in a vase, Luc pulled out a big pot and a bag of spaghetti.

"I'll make dinner tonight," he said and began filling the pot with water. When she hesitated as if she might refuse, he added, "You have to eat, I have to eat. You set the table while I boil the noodles. Spaghetti with an authentic Italian sauce—" he pulled a jar of ready-made sauce from the cupboard and hoisted it aloft "—is the one meal I can manage."

Julie smiled reluctantly and opened a cupboard to lift down the plates. They worked together, preparing the meal. She was still wary, Luc noted. When they bumped hips as he reached for the wine, she quickly stepped away.

But he played it cool. By the time they'd finished eating, Julie had relaxed enough to even chuckle at one of his jokes.

He picked up the wineglasses. "Let's finish these in the den," he said and stood up.

Julie hesitated, looking at the table. "But the dishes…"

"I'll do them later." Without giving her time to object, he headed toward the den. Puppy bustled right behind him.

Entering the room, Luc placed the glasses on the coffee table, then switched on the fireplace. He dimmed the lights while Puppy flopped down for his evening nap in front of the fire.

Then Luc sat on the couch and waited for Julie. He could hear her walking slowly down the hall. She appeared in the doorway, pausing to survey the softly lit room with all the caution of a deer examining a watering hole at nightfall.

She finally came in and walked toward the couch. But instead of sitting down in her usual spot next to him, she picked up her drink from the table and wandered off to look at his paintings.

Luc frowned. He stood and came up behind her.

She was studying his T. Novy collage, which featured a variety of figures set against a dark background of stars. While Julie gazed up at the painting, Luc gazed down at her. She'd twisted her hair up on top of her head in one of those knot things she liked, but as usual, a few unruly strands had worked loose to trail enticingly down her neck. His gaze lingered there, searching along the slim column of her throat for the mark he'd made…and finding it. The mark had faded to a barely discernible smudge on her white skin. He fought the urge to bend down and cover it with his mouth.

"What do all the figures symbolize?" Julie asked.

As she glanced his way, Luc jerked his gaze up to the painting. "They represent the various planets. Pluto, Mars and so on."

"Hmm." Sipping her wine, Julie studied the painting once more, her gaze on a wolf that appeared about to leap from the center of the canvas. Luc casually shifted closer…and she casually moved on again, walking slowly past the rest of his paintings to pause before his bookshelf.

Rats, foiled again, Luc thought. He prowled along behind her.

She set down her wineglass on the shelf and pulled out a thick black volume. Luc came up beside her, enjoying the way she frowned so seriously as she thumbed through the book. He watched her slender finger skim slowly down a page, imagining how that finger would feel skimming along his skin, down his chest and stomach to his—

"You like this?"

"Huh? Well, I—" *Oh. She was referring to the book.* He glanced at the title. *Real Estate Investment Trust Management.* "It's okay. Not especially exciting, but necessary for my work."

She slid it back into the case and scanned the other titles. "What do you read for pleasure?"

He shrugged. "I don't really read for pleasure."

No surprise there, Julie thought. No doubt he was too busy doing *other things* for pleasure.

She retrieved her drink and started to step away, then pulled up short when a small, silver frame caught her eye. Tucked in a corner of the shelf, the old-fashioned filigree piece looked totally out of place against the stark, plain business tomes lined up behind it.

Intrigued, Julie picked the picture up for a better look. She studied the image behind the glass. A thin, gray-haired little old lady stared back at her with Luc's dark chocolate eyes. She was clothed all in black, with her gloved hands folded sedately in her lap. Her face was set in stern lines. Yet a hint of humor sparkled in her deep-set eyes, and her thin lips were pursed, as if she suppressed a smile.

Julie gave Luc a questioning look.

"My aunt. My late Aunt Sophia, who gave Puppy to me," he told her and turned away.

Julie watched him stroll back to the couch to sit down. He caught her eye, and patted the spot beside him. "C'mon, Julie. Sit down."

He slouched back in his seat, waiting for her to respond.

And Julie knew how she *should* respond: she should march out the door. After last night, she hadn't intended to even see Luc this evening, let alone have dinner with him. And she certainly hadn't intended to sit on that couch with him—not ever again!

But she was curious about his aunt. This was the only picture he'd put out of any of his relatives. And this was the woman who'd owned Puppy. Still holding the frame in her hand, she walked over and sat down at the other end of the couch, her curiosity piqued. "Tell me about her, Luc."

His eyes gleamed as she'd drawn near, but his lids half lowered at her question, shielding his gaze. "Not much to tell." He picked up the remote and flicked on the TV.

"She looks interesting," Julie said.

"She was okay. Old-fashioned, but fair."

"Were you close?"

"Yeah. Kind of." He glanced at her. Julie met his gaze expectantly. With a sigh, he flicked off the television and set down the remote. "My parents were killed in a car accident when I was in my last year of high school. She brought me out here from New York to live with her."

Julie bit her lip. "I'm sorry."

He shrugged, but there was a slight tension in his shoulders. "Stuff happens."

"Still, it must have been hard."

"Probably harder for her than for me. She was broke, living on a small pension. Since my parents hadn't taken out insurance, it wasn't easy to make ends meet."

"How did she do it?"

"By counting every penny and working hard."

"Did she resent you for it?"

"No. Not at all. Family meant everything to her. And she was determined to do her best by me." A reluctant smile curved his mouth. "I thought I was big stuff, a real man at seventeen. She sure set me straight. She was only five foot nothing, but she had me quaking in my size twelve work boots when I told her I was going to get a job instead of going to college. She valued hard work, but she valued an education even more. She wouldn't hear of it."

Julie looked down at the picture. "So what did you do?"

He shrugged again. "I did both. Worked construction during the day, went to college at night and eventually became a developer." He reached over, and plucked the picture from her hands. He set it on the coffee table, then turned to face her. "So what about you?"

"Me?"

"Yeah, you. How did you come to own the Puppy Love Dog Training Institute?"

"Oh, that. I got lucky," Julie said. She stared at Aunt Sophia's face a moment longer. She wanted to talk more about the woman. It seemed his aunt had loved Luc very much. But he obviously didn't want to talk about her anymore. So, with a sigh, Julie scooted back into the corner of the couch, curled her legs under her to get comfortable and folded her empty hands in her lap. "I wanted to be a veterinarian, so when my parents moved back east to be closer to my brother and his family, I stayed here to go to college and began working at the institute to earn extra money. I soon discovered that I wasn't cut out to be a vet." She shook her head wryly. "It hurt too much when an animal died—or had to be put down. But training them was something I truly enjoyed. So, when the previous owner decided she wanted to sell, I put down the money my grandparents had left me, took out a loan for the rest and—" she spread out her hands "—there you go."

"Very impressive."

Not really, Julie thought. She'd never been the successful one in her family; she hadn't tried to be. She'd learned early that no matter what she did, in her parents' eyes, she'd always come in second to her brother. And she certainly couldn't claim to have been anywhere near as financially successful as Luc had been. She glanced around at the expensive furniture and the artwork on the walls. His business was obviously thriving, while she was dog-paddling madly to simply stay afloat.

She shifted restlessly at the thought. She should go work on the books—instead of courting trouble by hanging out here with Luc.

Uncurling her legs, she rose to her feet. "I'd better get going."

His dark eyebrows lifted in surprise. "So early?"

"Yes. I have some accounts I need to go over."

"That's usually my line." He stood up, too, and gave a huge stretch, long muscular arms reaching toward the ceiling. When his arms came down, one landed around her shoulders, holding her in place with a casual hug. "Want some help?"

With his steely arm around her, Julie glanced up at his face. The firelight played over the lean planes of his cheeks and revealed the gleam in his heavy-lidded dark eyes as they met hers. Yes, she did want his help, she realized. Luc was an expert at business. He could probably tell her exactly what she was doing wrong with the institute.

But asking for his help wouldn't be smart.

Because she'd lied when she'd told him she didn't want him. She knew it and—judging by the glint in his eyes—he knew it, too. But that was just too bad.

Perhaps wanting Luc had been inevitable. Loving him, however, was something she simply couldn't allow herself to do.

So, she needed to keep him out of her personal life, and her business life, as well.

"No, thank you," she said politely. "I can manage."

His arm tightened slightly, and then he released her with a shrug. "Whatever you say."

And Julie escaped from the room.

She tried to avoid Luc during the next few days and was carefully polite whenever she ran into him. But on

Saturday, he surprised her by stopping in her office at the institute right after Puppy's class.

With Puppy at his heels, he caught her with her elbows on her desk, one finger twisting a strand of her hair as she leaned forward, staring at the computer screen.

"I thought I'd pick up a pizza for dinner," Luc said as she looked up.

"I'm going to be a while—"

"No problem. I'll have it delivered here," he replied and pulled out his cell phone to punch in a number before she could protest further.

Julie still didn't intend to let Luc help her with her finances, but somehow, by the time the pizza arrived, he was sitting at her desk frowning over the accounts, while she hovered by his broad shoulder answering questions and Puppy napped in a corner.

It didn't take Luc long to reach a conclusion. "To put it simply, other than a few tax deductions you haven't taken advantage of, and some rather creative accounting, the major mistake you've been making is failing to pass your increasing costs along to your clients. From what I can see, you haven't raised your fees in the past two years."

"I already charge quite a bit—"

"What you charge needs to be determined by your expenses, plus a healthy profit. For example, when your rent goes up, your fees need to rise to cover the increase."

"Or I can take a decrease in profit."

"Yeah, you could do that," he agreed dryly. "Except in your case, your profit is already so slim, it's almost nonexistent."

While Luc paused to let that sink in, he picked up a

slice of pizza. Tearing off a bite, he leaned back in his chair to study Julie's face while he chewed. She looked serious and concerned—but not too surprised. Which didn't surprise him in the least. She'd probably known exactly what the problem was all along. But with her soft heart, she just hadn't wanted to admit it.

"You're going to have to get tough," he told her. "When it comes to business, it's a dog-eat-dog world. You should always collect your fees in advance, and no more giving people a break. From what I can see, you've neglected to charge at least five people for this past session alone."

"Those are scholarships."

"Financed by you—when you really can't afford it."

She crossed her arms, and leaned her bottom against the desk, not entirely convinced. "I'll raise my fees—and collect them in advance," she conceded. "But some clients just don't have the money to come to classes—and it's important for the benefit of their animals that they do."

Luc heaved an exasperated sigh at her serious, stubborn expression. "Look, Julie, you and I both know that if these people don't have the know-how or the money to train their pet properly, then they shouldn't own a dog. And if you want your business to grow, and to expand in the future—"

"I don't."

"What?"

"I want my business to be profitable, but I don't want to expand."

"What do you mean, you don't want to expand?" he demanded. "You could make more money."

"That's not my goal. My goal is to help owners train their dogs—and to work with them one-on-one. I like the institute just the way it is. As you can see," she added, gesturing at the computer, "management and paperwork are hardly my forte. Training dogs—and their owners— is. So that's what I want to do. Not be stuck in an office as an overseer. I also want a life outside of work."

Julie suppressed a smile at the expression on Luc's face. He couldn't have appeared more stunned if she'd announced she was going to abandon the institute and start grooming cats for a living. But although his reaction made Julie want to smile, it also saddened her. Because it was just another indication of how different they were.

Which brought to mind a topic she'd been trying not to think about. Absently, she shut the lid on the pizza. Squaring her shoulders, she looked over at Luc to find him watching her.

"Luc…"

"Yeah?"

"Our agreement is almost finished. Puppy has finished with basic training. And my apartment will be ready on Wednesday."

Luc gave her a sharp glance. "That soon?"

She nodded.

He frowned at the dog sleeping in the corner. "But Puppy still acts up at times. He isn't ready for you to leave yet."

"There are still a couple of things I'd like to work with him on," she admitted. "And I'll do that in the next couple days. But for the most part, I think everything's worked out nicely, don't you?"

"Yeah. I suppose," Luc said vaguely.

But he really didn't think so.

He discussed the subject with Puppy as they drove home behind Julie's little red Volkswagen.

"So, what do you make of all this?" he asked the dog. "It sure doesn't sound like she's ready to adopt you, does it? Or sleep with me," he added, staring broodingly at the taillights of the little car up ahead.

Puppy didn't bother to answer. He thrust his muzzle out the half-open window to scent the air.

"This isn't something you can ignore," Luc warned him, glancing in his direction. "After all, it's your future that's at stake here, too."

Puppy pulled his head back inside the truck to look at him.

"It's true," Luc insisted. "I've never met a woman so stubborn. It's damn frustrating the way she keeps me at a distance. My gut tells me that if this isn't settled before I leave for Costa Rica, I'll never see her again. But every time I take two steps forward, she dances three steps out of reach."

Puppy sat up straighter. He whined a little and shifted in the seat. He panted happily.

"Yeah, I know. She's still a pushover when it comes to you," Luc agreed grudgingly.

He thought that over. It was the answer; he could sense it. "That's the key," he said thoughtfully. "*You're* the key."

Puppy barked, then barked again a little louder.

Letting go of the wheel, Luc reached over to rub the mastiff's big broad head. "Yeah, if we work on her together, maybe we can both get what we want."

Chapter Nine

On dogs and history:

During the rise of the Roman Empire, fighting
was a way of life. Mars, the Roman god of war,
was the most worshipped deity throughout the
ancient civilization. Due to his military associa-
tion, Mars was regarded as the people's protector. He was commonly portrayed in full battle
armor with his sacred animal, the wolf, by his
side. Whereas Venus ruled romantic attraction,
Mars represented raw energy, aggressive action
and lustful, sexual attraction—the basic, animal
nature of man.

In emulation of this revered hero, Roman warriors girded their loins, donned their helmets and
trained their massive dogs for battle. Utilizing
physical strength and animal cunning, the brutes

entered a conflict side by side, determined to gain
their objectives.
Historic Hounds, Benedict Barbar

The next morning, Julie drank her coffee black. She
needed it strong, and she needed it now.

She yawned and set down her cup. Resting her
elbow on the small table in the guesthouse, she
propped her chin in her hand. Once again, Luc had
prevented her from getting a good night's sleep.
Thoughts of him had kept her awake, and when she
finally managed to drop off, he'd invaded her dreams.
Dressed like a Roman gladiator, wolfish smile on his
face and spear in hand—how Freudian was that?—
he'd pursued her with relentless determination
through the institute obstacle course, with Puppy barking at his heels.

Julie shuddered and picked up her coffee cup again
to take a deep gulp. This obsession with the man had
to stop. Thank goodness she'd be moving soon and—

A sharp knock made her jump. Standing up, she
tightened the sash on her cotton robe and went to answer the door.

Luc and Puppy were standing outside. Luc's gaze
skimmed down her body, and Julie automatically tightened her sash again as she examined his own outfit. Her
gaze roamed over his muscular arms revealed by his
sleeveless white T-shirt, his long legs clad in faded
jeans, down to scuffed tennis shoes and back up to his
determined expression.

"We need to bathe Puppy," he said.

"We do?" Julie said doubtfully.

"Yeah," Luc insisted. "We either need to bathe him,
or change his name to Old Smeller."

"Oh, please…"

"Oh, please nothing. Let's face it, Julie, the mutt stinks."

"He's not a mutt. And he simply smells like a dog."

"Yeah, a dirty dog. He needs a bath. Besides—" he glanced down at Puppy, who returned the look with a suspicious stare "—it'll cool him off. It's gonna be a scorcher today."

"But I thought I'd go into work—"

She broke off as Puppy lifted his back leg to give himself a brisk scratch.

Julie stared at the mastiff in faint horror. "Oh, my goodness, I hope he doesn't have fleas!" She put her hands under Puppy's jowls and lifted his head to meet his eyes. "Do you need a bath, Puppy?"

Puppy wagged his stubby tail perfunctorily, but didn't seem overly thrilled about the idea. But Julie was convinced. She gave Puppy's head a pat and told Luc, "Okay. Let me get dressed, and I'll be right out."

She shut the door.

Luc gave Puppy a look of approval. "Not bad. That scratching was a nice touch." Pleased, he led Puppy around to the side of the house where he'd left a pail, some sponges and a bottle of dog shampoo.

He'd slipped off Puppy's collar, and was filling the bucket with the hose when Julie joined them, dressed in shorts, flip-flops and a faded Institute T-shirt. Luc stared at her cute little toes with their polished pink nails and smiled.

"You're not going to use cold water, are you?" she demanded, drawing his gaze to her frowning face. "We should heat some water to wash him with."

"It's ninety degrees out here. He'll probably love getting wet by the hose."

Puppy tolerated the initial soaking—and even remained still as Julie worked the dog shampoo into his short, dense brown coat. "Good boy," she said as she scrubbed. She glanced at Luc, who stood watching. "You could help here."

"You're doing fine."

"But this was your idea, and—good boy—no, Puppy—no!" She shrieked as the dog suddenly shook himself, spraying watery suds all over her. "Puppy, stay still!"

Puppy obeyed—but stood quivering, clearly wanting to shake again.

Julie wiped suds off her cheek with the back of her hand, and gave Luc—who'd remained at a safe distance—a baleful look.

He chuckled and picked up the hose. "Here. I'll rinse him off."

Puppy quivered under that even more. But Luc had almost finished when Puppy made a break for it. Slipping out of Julie's grip, the mastiff trotted away.

"Puppy!" Luc yelled. "Get back here!"

But Puppy rounded the corner of the house and disappeared.

"Coward," Luc said, throwing down the hose in disgust. "Afraid of a little water."

Julie put her hands on her hips. "Maybe he just doesn't like being doused with suds or having freezing cold water sprayed on him. I told you we should have heated some water."

"It's not that cold."

"Isn't it?" Impulsively, she picked up the hose. Aiming the water in Luc's direction, she let him have it full blast. "Then how do you like it?"

He howled in surprise. Julie laughed. She got him

good. In less than five seconds, he was soaked. Shirt. Jeans. Shoes.

Turning the hose aside, she laughed again at the astounded expression on Luc's face. He stood with his arms stretched out, water dripping from his head down to his feet.

He stared down at his wet clothes, then back up at her. And the wicked glint in his eyes made her drop the hose to start backing slowly away.

"Now, Luc." She bit her underlip to keep from laughing and held up her hands. "I just wanted to make a point. Don't get mad."

"Mad?" He started pacing toward her. "You're forgetting I'm Italian, Julie. We're the kind that just gets even."

She backed away more quickly. "I'm sorry."

"You're gonna be."

He stopped, grabbed the edge of his soaked T-shirt and whipped it up and over his head. He flung it aside.

Julie's breath caught in her throat. His chest was wide and hard, with muscles rippling beneath his gleaming brown skin. The light dusting of hair on his torso arrowed down his taut abdomen into his jeans. He looked wild, dangerous.

And he was out to get *her*.

Julie tried to hold her ground. To remain calm. She sensed that if she didn't, things would rapidly escalate out of control.

But Luc took another step toward her. And the cheerful, anticipatory menace on his hard face made her heart beat faster in half-fearful excitement.

"Stop, Luc," she ordered.

He took another step closer.

"I mean it."

"So do I." He reached out to grab her—and she broke and ran.

He chased her. Half panicked, half laughing help-lessly, Julie sprinted across the yard. She felt his touch on her shoulder. She shrieked and circled a hedge. He came around the other way. She dodged his long arms, squealing in protest, "No, Luc. Stop! I'm sorry."

Her breath soon came in short, excited pants. Laugh-ter and excitement weakened her. Julie dimly sensed he could have caught her at any time, that he was playing with her, getting close enough, touching her just enough, to send her into panicked sprints, but she wasn't thinking very clearly. Instinct had taken over. She was the hunted; he was the hunter.

But he wasn't going to catch *her*.

She turned to face him down, holding out her hands and putting on a determined expression. "Now, Luc," she said firmly—and he tackled her.

Julie shrieked as he lifted her off her feet. The sky spun dizzily over her head in midair, and she landed with a thump. Right on Luc.

She wasn't hurt. Just breathless from laughter and the impact with his hard body. He'd wrapped his arms around her as they fell, his big body cushioning hers, leaving her sprawled across him. But before she could push away, his arms tightened and he rolled, pinning her to spongy turf.

Her lower body cradled his, his chest flattened her breasts. He raised his chest slightly off hers and caught her wrists, pinning them to the ground on either side of her head. Then he lifted his head to look down into her laughing face. "Now I've got you."

She tried to sound firm. "Luc, get off me."

"Say you're sorry."

She eyed his expression, then bit her lip. He buried his face in the crook of her neck and shoulder, growling menacingly against her sensitive skin.

She squealed and hunched her shoulder, trying to escape. "Luc! That tickles! I'm sorry! *I'm sorry!*"

He lifted his head to stare down into her eyes. "I don't believe you."

"It's true."

He settled his hips more firmly against hers. "You're a liar, Julie Jones."

His voice sounded husky. Julie's laughter died. The sunlight haloed his head, shadowing his features. A hot flush rose under her skin at the intent, possessive expression on his face. The predatory gleam in his eyes.

Her heart beat faster. "I'm not a liar."

"Yes, you are." He lowered his head, and his voice grew huskier. "And I'm going to prove it."

He kissed her mouth. Lightly. Then more deeply— longer. Julie's eyes fluttered shut as she parted her lips beneath his. He released her hands, but she let them lie limp. The grass felt cool and prickly against her back and bare legs. Luc's wet jeans were ice-cold where they pressed against the front of her thighs. But the smooth skin of his chest and flat belly was warm, so warm.

He slid his hand through her hair, cradling her head in his palm. He turned her face to angle his mouth even more firmly against hers. He kissed her deeply, intently, as if he meant to consume her—blurring her thinking. His heat surrounded her. His hot mouth and tongue branded her. Logic fled, replaced by the feel of his hard chest pressed against her breasts—his bare, hair roughened skin rubbing against her through the thin cotton of her T-shirt, the silk of her bra. Her nipples peaked as he slowly brushed against them, and she wrapped her arms around him to trace the contoured muscles of his back, feel his smooth skin beneath her fingers.

He broke the kiss, his hot mouth skimming across her cheek, down to her neck. Julie shivered with excitement. "Ah, babe, you taste so sweet," he muttered against her throat, punctuating the words with tiny, stinging kisses. "I've never wanted anyone as much as I want you."

Luc felt Julie quiver beneath him. He slid his hand beneath her damp T-shirt and bra to cup her breast. Her nipple stabbed his palm and hot, hard heat surged through him. He inhaled harshly. The sharp, herbal scent of the dog shampoo on her clothes mingled with the scent of the grass, and he buried his nose against her neck again, seeking the delicate, sweeter scent of her skin.

He kissed her throat, then covered her mouth again with increasing urgency. Operating solely on animal instinct, he pressed his hips firmly against her, responding to her scent, her softness and the promise of sexual release she provided. He nipped at her swollen bottom lip, then laved its plump softness, saying thickly, "C'mon, sweetheart. Let's go into the house."

For Julie, the words didn't register for a moment. She uttered an instinctive moan of protest as he suddenly lifted himself off her. Feeling bereft, she blinked her eyes open, lifting her hand to shield them against the glare of the sun.

Luc was standing above her, the sun behind his head. He reached down. He caught her upper arms and lifted her easily, setting her on her feet.

Julie stood there shakily. She felt confused. Disoriented. Automatically, she pulled down the hem of her T-shirt and glanced up at Luc. Her gaze lingered on the slight smile curving his lips, then lifted to his eyes. His skin had pulled taut over his hard features and the hot, unmasked desire in his dark brown eyes made her flush.

She glanced away, trying to get her bearings, feeling as if she'd just woken up after a vivid dream. Her gaze landed on the running hose and abandoned bottle of shampoo. "Where's Puppy?"

Luc's expression shifted, then hardened. His lips tightened and he took her hand. "He's around. We'll check on him later."

He started to lead her toward the house, but Julie balked, pulling away from his grasp. "No. I want to make sure he's okay."

She started walking toward the guesthouse, aware that Luc made an impatient sound before he followed her. She could almost feel the angry, gathering tension emanating from him as he stalked silently at her heels. She knew that he thought checking on Puppy was just an excuse to halt what was happening between them. And he was half-right. She was scared, uncertain, of the desire that burned between them. That kiss had moved so fast—Luc was moving so fast. She needed to slow this down. She needed to think.

But she also needed to find Puppy. To make sure he was all right. Not that there was any reason for him not to be. But Luc had yelled at him. And Puppy hadn't come back.

They found the mastiff in his crate. He'd crawled in soaking wet on top of the blanket used for his bedding. "We're going to have to wash his blanket," Julie said.

Luc didn't respond.

Julie crouched down beside the crate. "C'mon out, big boy," she coaxed. "C'mon Puppy."

Puppy just looked at her. Julie sighed. Now she had two sulking males to deal with. She said more demandingly, "Puppy, come."

Puppy shifted and made a sound—whether it was a whimper or a growl, Julie couldn't tell, but Luc said sharply. "He doesn't like anyone near his crate."

"It's okay," Julie said.

She gave the Puppy the command again—at the same time Luc did. And she wasn't sure if it was her voice or Luc's sterner tone that the dog responded to, but Puppy rose and left the kennel to stand by their side.

"Good boy," Julie praised Puppy softly, scratching his neck. "We need to get you rinsed off and dried."

Luc just strode over to the crate and yanked out the blanket Puppy had been lying on. Something else fell out, as well.

A small, black rag.

Luc stared down at it for a long silent moment. Then he bent and picked it up. Julie felt Puppy tense beneath her hand. She thought the dog might lunge, but Puppy simply sat there, watching intently as Luc turned the black rag over in his hand.

"What is it?" Julie asked, puzzled by the expression on his face.

For a moment, he didn't answer. And when he did, his voice sounded husky. "It's a glove. My aunt's glove. She lost it about three years ago when she came to visit." He looked up and met her eyes. Julie was stunned at the pain in his gaze. "Puppy must have found it somewhere in the house."

"Maybe—in the couch?" Julie suggested hesitantly.

"Maybe," Luc agreed.

He glanced at Puppy, sitting stiffly erect by Julie's side. "Come here, boy," he commanded quietly.

Puppy hesitated, then walked over to Luc's side. He nudged the man's hand.

Luc held out the glove.

Gently, very gently, Puppy took it in his massive jaws.

Luc reached down and lifted the wide muzzle to look into the dog's big brown eyes. "So that's what the problem is. You've been grieving for her, haven't you?"

Julie watched them, her chest tightening at the look on Luc's face.

Luc released the dog's muzzle to place his hand on the animal's broad, faithful head. It bowed beneath his touch. Puppy's eyes closed as Luc gently scratched behind his ears—the place the dog loved.

And Luc's expression softened. "I know. I know, boy," he said gently. "I miss her, too."

And—just like that—Julie fell in love with Luc Tagliano.

Chapter Ten

The canine spirit:

The ancients viewed dogs as messengers between the living and the dead. The canines' spiritual journeys occurred most often during the "dog days of summer," when the brightest light in the night sky—Sirius, the Dog Star—rose and set with the sun.

Today's philosophers postulate that the dog inhabits the netherworld between the human and the nonhuman; a lowly beast imbued with the divine qualities of loyalty and unquestioning love.
Canine Kindred Souls, Don Lee Marian

The realization that she loved Luc exhilarated Julie. It frightened her, too.

For the next twenty-four hours, she seesawed between emotional extremes—one second, filled with happiness; the next, filled with fear. Luc had been preoccupied after Puppy had given up the glove and had retired to his office. That had been fine with her. She holed up in the guesthouse to try to think things over. She wasn't sure of anything—except that she couldn't tell Luc how she felt.

Because she had no idea how he felt about her. All right, he wanted her—even a dog with its head down a gopher hole could tell that. There was no mistaking that look in his eyes, the heat in his gaze.

But he'd wanted other women in the past. There was no doubt about that, either. Those sultry female voices were no longer coming on the message machine, but that didn't mean those women still didn't exist. She wondered if he'd loved any of those women in his past. She didn't think so.

But he'd changed. He'd settled down during these last six weeks. He'd bonded with Puppy and—she couldn't help believing—with her. He'd even said he'd never wanted another woman as much as he did her. The memory made her shiver. Surely, he wouldn't have said that, wouldn't look at her with such tenderness, such intensity, if he didn't care for her? Surely, it was safe to take the risk of giving in to the growing desire between them. Because maybe if their physical relationship deepened, their emotional connection would deepen, as well.

She was still pondering the dilemma, trying to decide which path to take, the next evening while she waited for Luc to get home for dinner.

She'd made stew again. She smiled faintly as she looked down at the meat browning in the pan. "This is people stew," she told Puppy, who was sitting by her side, looking hopeful. "You've already had yours."

Puppy remained close, though, as she laid the table and put candles in the middle. It was as if he could sense something important was going to happen. And it would, Julie decided. Tonight, she and Luc would definitely talk about where their relationship was headed. Whether they talked before or after they made love— her heart leaped into her throat—depended on the circumstances.

Butterflies fluttered in her stomach, and she pressed a hand against her middle to settle them down. Wine, she thought. A special night like tonight deserves wine. And it would help calm her nerves.

She'd just put the wine on the table when the phone rang.

Julie sighed. "It's probably Luc—calling to say he'll be a little late," she grumbled to Puppy. But when she picked up the receiver, it wasn't Luc that responded to her hello.

"Hello, is this the Luc Tagliano residence?" a woman inquired.

Julie heart sank. Not another "old friend." "Yes," she replied politely, "This is. But Luc isn't here right now. May I take a message?"

"Oh, yes," the woman said. "I'm calling in regard to the ad he placed in the newspaper…"

Julie's mood lightened. Not a past lover, then.

"The ad concerning the mastiff he has. The purebred *Cane corso* mastiff with papers?"

Julie frowned in puzzlement. "There's an ad in the newspaper about his dog?"

"Yes. *The Los Angeles Times,*" the woman assured her. "He hasn't placed the dog yet, has he?"

"Well, no, but there must be some mistake. Mr. Tagliano had been looking for a home for the dog, but

I'm afraid he's decided to keep him. The paper probably ran the ad again in error," she added, positive that's what had happened.

"Oh." The syllable was filled with disappointment, and a faint suspicion. "Are you sure?"

"Positive."

"Well, I'm sorry to hear that." The woman sighed, then added more briskly, "But would you mind taking down my number anyway? Just in case he changes his mind again?"

"Of course not," Julie replied and dutifully wrote down the woman's name and number. Not that it would do any good, she thought as she hung up the phone. Luc wouldn't be giving away Puppy. But he would need to inform the paper about their mistake and make sure the ad got pulled this time. She made a mental note to remind him as soon as he got home.

But when Luc arrived few minutes later, she forgot about the call.

"Julie?" he called as he came in the front door. "You here?"

"In the kitchen."

A few seconds later, he strode into the kitchen. Standing by the stove, she glanced over her shoulder at him. He'd taken off his jacket and loosened his tie. His face had lost that solemn, rather stern look he'd worn yesterday after Puppy had given up the glove. He looked relaxed again—and that hot gleam of desire was back in his eyes. He paused in the middle of the room, eyeing her as he rolled up his cuffs.

"Hi," she said, almost shyly.

"Hi, yourself."

The look in his eyes made her heart beat faster, and she hurriedly turned back to her cooking. "Are you hungry?"

"Ravenous," he replied and slid his arms around her waist. Pulling her back against him, he nuzzled the sensitive place under her ear with his sandpapery jaw, then nipped at her ear, making her jump.

"Luc!" Her pulse was racing, but she hid her reaction with a reproving look. "Sit down. Dinner's almost ready."

"Man, I love a domineering woman," he growled against her neck, sending more shivers up her spine. He squeezed her more tightly, then released her. "Especially a domineering woman who can cook."

He reached past her for a piece of stew meat in the pan—and she rapped his fingers lightly with the spoon.

"Ow!"

She ignored his injured look and pointed at a chair with the spoon. "Sit!"

Luc sat—after he'd opened the wine and filled the glasses. Then he dug into the stew with relish. Julie watched him eat, so pleased with his obvious enjoyment of her cooking, so busy listening to him talk about his day—that it wasn't until they'd finished their meal that she remembered about the phone call.

"She saw an ad saying Puppy was still available," Julie told him. "The paper must have run your earlier ad again by mistake."

Luc was leaning back, toying with the stem of his wine glass, his gaze fixed on her face. "They didn't make a mistake," he said idly. "Sounds like I finally found him a home."

Julie was sure she must have misheard. "You're giving Puppy away?"

He caught her hand. Lifting it to his mouth, he kissed each of her fingers, one by one. "Not if you want him, of course."

He nibbled on the tips of her fingers, his gaze growing warmer as he looked at her in the candlelight.

Julie shook her head. "I told you. I have nowhere to keep him."

"So stay in the guesthouse. It's worked out well, hasn't it? And you still wouldn't have to pay any rent. That would certainly cut your expenses. You'd be with Puppy—" his voice lowered to a huskier note, and he leaned toward her, his heavy lids drooping over his eyes "—and you and I could spend some time together, whenever I'm at home. It's the perfect solution all around."

"Perfect for you, maybe." Her voice sounded cool, but her stomach twisted with a sickening feeling of déjà vu. She'd been here before—had this conversation with Luc the first day she'd met him. He hadn't wanted Puppy then, either. But she'd thought he'd changed.

Well, he obviously hadn't. Not about Puppy. Nor, she was afraid, in his attitude about women. His attitude about her.

Her hands felt cold. She pulled free of his hold and clasped them tightly together on the table, squeezing until her fingers went numb. Her lips felt numb, too, as she said, "Luc, if you don't have time in your life for Puppy, then how can you have time in your life for me?"

"For God's sake, what does one thing have to do with the other?" he said impatiently. "He's a dog—he can't understand why I'm not here when I'm off on a business trip or working late. But you would."

She kept her tone level. "So that's what you're planning? To start traveling? Working longer hours again?"

Luc reached out to grasp her hands again, folding them in his. "I have to. After spending all this time with Puppy, I need to catch up. I'll be traveling to Costa

Rica at the end of this week, and I'm scheduled to be in Italy by the end of next month."

"You'll be busy, all right."

His hands tightened on hers, and his eyes softened. "Yeah, I'll be busy, but don't worry. I'll make time in my life for you."

A shaft of pain cut through Julie's chest. She stared at him silently, her heart aching. She'd wondered about his past relationships, if he'd loved one of those women who'd contributed to that masculine confidence that went bone deep. Now she knew he hadn't. Not then…and not now.

He'd said that she was special. But she wasn't, it seemed, quite special enough.

She took a deep breath, trying to ease the growing tightness in her chest. Eyes burning but dry, she met his gaze. "I don't want a man who will make time in his life for me," she said quietly. "I want a man who will make me his life."

He frowned, his dark eyes narrowing in angry confusion. But before he could reply, she pulled free of his grasp and stood up.

She stepped forward blindly; something bumped against her side. She glanced down at Puppy.

He met her gaze, his big eyes worried. Whining, he thrust his muzzle against her hand. He licked her palm, then nuzzled it again.

Offering comfort, seeking it.

Julie crouched down. She wrapped her arms around his thick neck and buried her face against his fur. The warm bulk of his big body gave her something solid to lean on, if only for a moment.

Her arms tightened. She gave Puppy a final hug, then rose and headed toward the door.

"Julie," Luc growled, pushing back his chair to stand up, also. "Wait a minute. We can figure this thing out. Reach another agreement."

She didn't turn around.

His voice grew rougher. Angrier. "Is that all you know how to do? Run away? Withdraw into your own little world? Fine, then. Go. But don't blame this all on me, babe. Because every relationship requires compromises of some kind. From *both* parties involved."

But Julie kept going right out the door. Because she couldn't compromise. Not about this.

So there was nothing more to say.

Chapter Eleven

The antisocial animal:

Canines are typically social animals. The pack serves as their family, contributing not only to their physical well-being but their emotional health, as well.

Yet, the "lone wolf" syndrome is not a myth.

Wolves are genetically programmed not to accept strangers after six months of age. If their original pack members all die, some male wolves are caught in an emotional void. Unable to accept their loss, lacking the ability to create a new bond or commitment to others, they remain constantly on the move, traveling from territory to territory, living the rest of their lives alone.

This phenomenon is known to exist in some dogs, as well.
The Wandering Wolf, Dr. Al Tuttle

Luc drove Puppy to his new home the next day.

He pulled up at the house and switched off the engine. He sat in silence for a moment, then glanced at the mastiff sitting quietly on the seat beside him.

Puppy didn't look at him, but stared at the windshield with somber dignity.

Luc's jaw tightened. "Look, she wants something I just don't have it in me to give. So she decided not to stay. Not for me. Not even for you. And there's nothing we can do but make the best of it. So, let's get this over with."

Luc got out of the car, walked around to the other side, then opened the door for Puppy to climb out, too. Then Luc paused, leash in his hand, to study the house in front of him. The homes in this area were expensive with big lots. Painted beige and trimmed with white, this place had no particular style but appeared almost painfully well-maintained. Hedges, precisely squared at the top, outlined the front of the property and bordered the cement walkway leading straight to the front door.

Luc strode up the narrow walk. Puppy paced by his side. They reached the white door, and Luc pushed the doorbell.

A woman answered. Her red hair was clipped short in a boxy style that reminded Luc of her hedges.

"Mrs. Kepley?"

Her suspicious gaze skipped from his face to the mastiff beside him and back again. Her sharp features tightened with a smile. "Yes, I'm Irene Kepley. And you must be Luc Tagliano." She looked at Puppy again. "And this must be the *Cane corso* you mentioned in the ad. Primus Del Colosseo."

"Actually, he prefers to be called Puppy."

The woman didn't appear to hear him. Her attention was fixed on the dog, her gaze busily running over him from broad head to stubby tail. "He's certainly big! I was hoping he'd be a brindle," she admitted, "but although his coat is rather a commonplace color, it's very dense and shiny. I'm almost positive that with a lot of hard work, I can turn him into a champion." She gave Luc an inquiring look. "You said he's three years old, if I remember correctly. That he hasn't been altered and has his papers?"

"Yeah."

The woman gave a satisfied nod. "How are his teeth?"

"Sharp."

She stared blankly at Luc, then back at the dog. "Well, he certainly appears sound and healthy."

"Yeah. He is." Luc absently wrapped the leash around his fist. "He likes to work out a lot. To take long walks on the treadmill or, better yet, on a leash. He eats good, too. And although he's not crazy about canned dog food he loves fresh stew meat. And vegetables— he's really into vegetables. Can't get enough. Pickles. Carrots—" Luc slapped the leash against his side in sudden frustration. "Damn. I forgot his carrot."

The woman's skinny eyebrows rose in bewilderment. "His carrot? I have some carrots—"

"Not those, the fake kind. It's his favorite toy. I gave him a cigar, too, but he never really took to it. Nor to his pacifier, but that's no surprise. And, damn—I forgot his glove, too. And his kennel." Luc half turned away. "Maybe I'd better go get—"

"No!" The woman reached out to stop him, catching his sleeve. "Really. There's no need. We have a dog run in the back of the property with a kennel for him."

"You have a dog run?"

"Yes. It's perfectly comfortable. Warm and dry, all year long. It's much easier than having such a big dog in the house. I'm sure Primus will just love it, won't you Primus?" she crooned at Puppy, who ignored her with aloof dignity. "I'll just get a check and—goodness, what am I thinking, keeping you standing out here?" She opened the door a little wider, revealing shiny wood floors and white carpet beyond. "Please come in while I get my checkbook—"

"No," Luc said abruptly. "I can't stay. And there's no need to pay me."

Her eyes brightened, but she protested, "Mr. Tagliano, this is an expensive dog. Are you sure?"

"Yeah."

Her smile widened. "Well, if you insist." She held out her hand for the leash.

Puppy looked up at Luc.

Luc looked down at Puppy. For a long moment, he stared into the dog's solemn brown eyes.

Then he abruptly looked away and gave the woman the leash.

"Thank you!" She tugged on the leather. "Come, Primus!"

Puppy hesitated, still looking at Luc. Then he lowered his head and followed her inside.

She shut the door.

Luc turned and quickly strode back to his truck. He climbed in. He leaned forward to put his key in the ignition, in a hurry to get back to—

His arm dropped.

Get back to what?

His palms were sweating, his hands shaking. He wiped them on his jeans, then clenched his fists around the steering wheel as he stared unseeingly out the windshield.

He'd fulfilled his obligation to his aunt. He'd found a home for the dog. No longer did he have to be home by a certain time to feed the mastiff. Or walk him. Or spend time with him. Once again, he was free to do whatever he wanted, whenever he wanted. In this whole world, there wasn't one other living being he had to care for. The house would stay clean and quiet. He could travel and stay away as long as he liked. He could work twenty-four hours a day if he chose to.

And no one would care.

He rested his forehead against the steering wheel. Julie wasn't there waiting for him to get home anymore. And now Puppy wouldn't be, either. He'd given away the last gift his aunt had left him. Because he knew— he'd always known deep in his heart—that Aunt Sophia considered Puppy a gift.

Because she'd loved that dog. And she'd loved Luc. And she'd wanted them to be together.

Luc's jaw tightened. He lifted his head and slammed out of the truck. He stalked up the narrow sidewalk leading straight to the door, jabbed the door bell, then gave the panels a couple hard knocks for good measure.

The red-haired woman opened it, a startled look on her face.

"I want my dog back," Luc told her.

"I've just put him in the backyard…" she started to protest, but Luc ignored her.

"Puppy!" he yelled. He curled his tongue and gave a piercing whistle. *"Puppy! Come here!"*

A muffled "woof" and then a crash could be heard in the back of the house, followed by the sound of a dog's claws scrabbling on a wooden floor. The woman turned with a gasp as Puppy came hurtling toward her down the hallway. She stepped aside just before Puppy flew past.

He headed straight for the truck.

The woman gasped again, pressing a hand against her chest. "He must have taken down my screen!"

"Send me the bill," Luc told her and turned away.

He strode quickly to the truck where Puppy sat waiting, opened the passenger door, then bent to pick up the dog. But before he could, Puppy leaped in.

All by himself.

The mastiff sat down on the seat. Lifting his head proudly, he looked at Luc and waited for praise.

"Good boy," Luc said, swallowing the lump in his throat. He patted the dog's head. "Good boy, Puppy."

He shut the door and strode around to the driver's side, climbed in and glanced at the mastiff sitting beside him.

Puppy looked back at him.

"Okay, pal." Luc started the truck. "Let's go get her."

Chapter Twelve

On dogs and men:

Some say the modern, domesticated dog is a parasite, living off the kindness of man. That we humanize our pets, treating them as people rather than animal.

What many fail to realize is the added dimension dogs provide in our lives. They teach us what it is to care for another living being. They teach us to enjoy the moment and the simple pleasures in life. They teach us the true meaning of unconditional love.

It's not so much that owners humanize their dogs, but rather that dogs humanize their owners.
A Human Animal, Nick Starten

Julie was at her desk, staring at her computer, when tiny, animated puppies suddenly appeared on the screen. They frolicked across the black background chasing a bouncing red ball. Julie blinked, then sighed. Once again, her computer had slipped into sleep mode as her mind slipped back into thoughts of Luc and the night before.

She flicked off the monitor. Why even bother trying to work? Shoving her ledger aside, she rested her forehead in her hands, trying to think things through. To get some clarity about everything that had happened. It was hard. Her head ached from staying up so late in her brand-new, barren apartment that she'd fled to from Luc's. And her heart ached even more from the pain of leaving him.

But he didn't love you, she reminded herself for at least the hundredth time that afternoon. *You did the right thing by walking away before he could hurt you more.*

She rubbed her temples, trying to ease the tension there. Had she been wrong to walk out? To refuse to compromise as he'd demanded? She just didn't know. It was in her nature to leave, to withdraw into herself in times of emotional stress. She'd done it even as a child. When her dog Sissy had died. Whenever her family moved. When she'd have to give back the puppies she'd fostered. When she'd realized that although her parents loved her, they loved her brother just a bit more.

She'd withdraw to escape the pain. And love, she'd learned at an early age, always meant pain. You couldn't have one without the other.

So she'd avoided love all these years. She hadn't pursued a serious relationship with a man. She kept friends at a distance. She didn't even own a pet.

She winced at the thought of how disapproving she'd

been of Luc's decision not to keep Puppy because he was too busy with work. Heck, she was no better. In fact, she was much, much worse. She *wanted* a dog, yet she didn't have one. Not, she realized with sudden painful clarity, because she couldn't afford to—if she made the changes Luc had advised for the institute, affording a better apartment that allowed pets would no longer be a problem at all. No, she didn't own a dog because she'd been trying to avoid being hurt. To avoid loving.

And it hadn't worked.

Because, despite all her caution, she loved Luc. And she loved Puppy, too.

She sighed, and pressed her palms harder against her eyes, making the darkness behind her lids deepen. She'd been right to walk away from the man, she decided. You couldn't make someone love you. She couldn't—*wouldn't*—spend her life trying to make Luc feel something that just wasn't there. If her childhood had taught her nothing else, she'd learned that love simply didn't work that way.

No, staying with Luc in a relationship based—on his part, at least—only on sex would only denigrate her own love. Accepting less than what she wanted from him would eventually destroy her soul.

But she'd been wrong to walk away from the mastiff. Because Puppy—*Puppy* was a different matter. The mastiff had loved her unconditionally. And she'd deserted him just when he'd needed her most.

She lifted her head and blinked her eyes open. She reached for the phone. Just as her fingers touched the receiver, a commotion erupted in the outer office and her door suddenly burst open.

Two magnificent Italian males filled her threshold. Georgia was right behind them, her face red with indignation. She elbowed her way past Luc and planted herself in front of his big frame.

"I tried to stop them," she told Julie, crossing her arms over her chest. "I told him you were working and wanted to be alone. But, as usual, he wouldn't listen." She glared at Luc threateningly over her shoulder.

He glared right back. "I told you I need to talk to her."

Georgia bristled. "Well, maybe *she* doesn't want to talk to *you*." She pushed her glasses up higher on her short nose and looked at Julie hopefully. "Would you like me to call the police?"

Julie met the trainer's eyes, and the concern she saw there comforted her bruised heart a little. Yes, Georgia was a good friend. Because somehow the other woman knew, without being told, exactly what Julie was feeling.

"No, Georgia. Of course we don't need the police," Julie said softly. She glanced at Luc, keeping her expression calm. "I'm sure this won't take long."

Georgia hesitated, then sighed. "Whatever you say," she said gruffly. And with a final sniff and glare at Luc, she left, shutting the door behind her.

Julie glanced at Luc again, then began to straighten the papers on her desk, trying to disguise the trembling of her hands. She'd hoped—prayed—that she wouldn't have to see him again so soon. That when she did see him, the pain she felt would have had time to ease.

It hadn't.

She straightened her shoulders. But she'd get through this. She had no choice. And now she could ask him for Puppy.

She looked at the mastiff. When she met his eyes, Puppy whined and bounced on his front paws, tugging at the leash. Luc released it and the big dog bustled toward her across the room, hind end wagging madly.

Julie turned in her chair to greet him, and Puppy slowed as he reached her side. He whined happily and nudged her arm.

Julie wrapped her arms around his neck and pressed her cheek against his fur. "Oh, Puppy. I've missed you so much," she whispered against him. Puppy whimpered happily, and she hugged him harder.

"I've found him a home," Luc said. "I wanted you to know."

Julie's arms tightened around the dog. She lifted her head and met Luc's eyes.

She'd opened her mouth to protest when he told her, "I've decided to keep him."

Julie's mouth snapped shut. The words hurt—she wanted Puppy. And yet, they made her happy, too. She'd always felt that the big man and the big dog belonged together. And she was glad Luc had learned to care about Puppy.

"That's good," she said finally. "I know you'll take good care of him."

"I'll do my best."

Julie nodded. Of course he would; he'd done that all along. Grieving inside, she slowly stroked Puppy's broad head, scratched behind his cropped ears. Puppy gave his dog purr, half closing his eyes in contentment as he rested his big head on her lap.

Luc came closer. He leaned against the side of her desk as he watched her pet the mastiff. "He loves you, you know."

"I know," Julie admitted.

"I love you, too."

Julie's hands stilled as she absorbed what Luc had

said. She felt as if the words tingled along her veins, making her pulse leap. She bit her lip. Hope warred with caution as she glanced up at his face, unsure whether to believe him or not.

The uncertainty in her eyes pierced Luc. His chest tightened. She looked tired and pale, with a sadness behind her calm expression that made his heart ache.

He'd hurt her. He was an ass.

He closed the final few feet between them. Pushing Puppy aside, he crouched by Julie's side and slipped his arm around her waist.

She leaned back and thrust out a hand as if to keep him away.

But Luc couldn't keep away. He captured her fingers in his and tightened his other arm around her. He looked down into her solemn gray gaze. "I love you so much, Julie. Without you, I'll always be lonely. When you left—when I finally realized today that I might never see you again—all I could think about was coming to find you. To beg you to please come back to me. To beg you to marry me—to love me, too." His voice deepened, darkened with intensity. "Do you think you could?"

She hid her face against his shoulder without answering, and Luc's heart dropped. He could feel her trembling and he buried his face against her hair. "You have to, Julie. You have to love me. Because you *are* my life. Nothing—nothing is more important to me than you are."

He kissed her temple, then her soft, flushed cheek. His voice husky, he whispered by her ear, "My house isn't a home without you in it. I want to take care of you, have babies with you. I want you with me always. I love you, Julie. Please tell me you love me."

Julie wanted to answer him. She couldn't. Her throat was too tight with happy tears.

She nodded—it wasn't enough. Not for Luc.

He growled impatiently, then kissed her mouth, deeply and passionately. "Talk to me," he demanded, against her lips. He held her away to look into her eyes. "Tell me you love me. Say it."

His dark eyes were filled with determination, desire—and more tenderness than Julie could ever have imagined.

She reached up to cradle his hard face in her hands. "I love you," she whispered.

His eyes darkened. His lids drooped half-shut, and a slow smile curved his mouth. He wrapped his arms around her, squeezing her tight. "Now tell me you'll marry me," he said thickly. He kissed her again. Then again. "Say yes."

"Yes," she said huskily, when she could speak.

And that was all he needed to hear.

E-Pawlogue

The Man wanted to leave.

The signs were obvious. His keys were in his hand, and he'd parked his mechanical beast right outside the front door. He kept trying to herd The Woman out to it.

She refused to be rushed. "Just let me make sure we haven't forgotten anything," she told him.

"We haven't," The Man declared.

Still, he paced patiently beside her as she slowly made her way from room to empty room.

I followed at their heels.

One year had passed—seven in dog time—since The Woman had moved into this house. She and The Man were mated now. In a ceremony held on the institute lawns before friends and her birth pack, they'd promised to remain together forever.

The Man obviously took the vow seriously. He'd always guarded The Woman carefully, but during the last couple of weeks he grew restless if she was out of his sight for too long.

Maybe because she moved so slowly these days. Maybe because her stomach had grown so round she'd told The Man, "I can't see my feet anymore."

She'd laughed when she said it. But I knew The Man worried about her. I worried, too.

So when he said, "Let's go, babe. I want to get there, and get you settled in and off your feet," I whined in agreement.

She smiled at me and then at The Man. "Quit hounding me, you two. I'm fine."

She paused in the doorway to the den. With her hand on her bulging stomach, she looked around the empty room. "I can't believe how quickly time has passed this last year." She slanted The Man a sidelong glance. "Or how quickly you got the other house ready for us to move in."

"Yeah," he agreed in a dry tone. "Getting that done was quicker than getting you out to the truck."

The Woman laughed and hit him lightly on the chest. He retaliated by wrapping his arms around her. She squirmed. He growled for her to be still. Then he began kissing her.

I sighed and laid down. This could take a while.

The Man lifted his head to murmur against her mouth, "Damn. I shouldn't have been so quick to have the bed moved."

The Woman chuckled and pulled away. "Okay. You've convinced me. Let's go."

They left the house, and I followed. The Man locked the front door, then he lifted The Woman into his mechanical beast. I sat, waiting politely while he leashed her in carefully, and gave her another kiss as he patted her belly.

Then he turned to me.

I froze. My muscles tensed.

He smiled. "Get in, Puppy!"

I jumped up on the seat.

The Woman draped her arm around me as we set out. I stuck my nose out the partially open window, enjoying the feel of the wind on my face. The Woman and The Man talked as we drove along, discussing a place called Costa Rica and the vacation home he planned to build there.

I didn't listen too closely to what they were saying. The scents from outside were pulling at me, prickling at my memory. Soon we turned into a cluster of houses, huddled against the hillside. I sniffed the air and shifted restlessly in my seat.

The Man glanced my way. "It's almost as if he knows where we're going."

"Of course he knows."

"Maybe I should have taken him along while I was working on the place."

The Woman shook her head. "No, I still think it's best we waited. It might have confused him, if we took him away again."

"I hope he'll be happy there."

"He will." She gave me a pat, then pressed her cheek against The Man's shoulder. "We all will." She touched her stomach and smiled. "It's such a lovely neighborhood to raise a family."

The Man pulled up in front of a house. He came around and opened my door.

I leaped out onto the grass. I stood there, quivering with joy.

I was *Home*.

I ran around the small front yard. The Woman

laughed as she watched me. And The Man laughed, too. I raced around them at top speed, barking madly, then took off down the brick path along the side of the house.

I snuffled eagerly along the grass, explored the hollow where I used to rest behind the hydrangea bush. My stride shortened and slowed when I reached the shady backyard, the place I remembered best.

The three oak trees there were tall and broad. They waved a gentle welcome at me and whispered softly in the breeze. Beneath them, the thin grass and damp earth felt cool against my paws. I padded around the yard, my muzzle lowered.

I searched for traces of Her scent.

Time shifted, and drifted away. I found the half-buried trowel she'd forgotten in the garden. I discovered an old pillow she'd left on the wooden swing. I coursed the area, tracking back and forth, but found nothing more.

She was gone.

Yet her voice, her scent were imprinted deep in my brain. And each stroke of her hand on my fur had touched my heart.

She'd left me behind. But she hadn't left me alone.

"Puppy!" I heard The Man and The Woman calling. "Puppy! Come here, boy!"

And I raced off to be with my family.

* * * * *

If you enjoyed what you just read,
then we've got an offer you can't resist!

Take 2 bestselling
love stories FREE!
Plus get a FREE surprise gift!

Clip this page and mail it to Silhouette Reader Service™

IN U.S.A.	IN CANADA
3010 Walden Ave.	P.O. Box 609
P.O. Box 1867	Fort Erie, Ontario
Buffalo, N.Y. 14240-1867	L2A 5X3

YES! Please send me 2 free Silhouette Romance® novels and my free surprise gift. After receiving them, if I don't wish to receive anymore, I can return the shipping statement marked cancel. If I don't cancel, I will receive 4 brand-new novels every month, before they're available in stores! In the U.S.A., bill me at the bargain price of $3.57 plus 25¢ shipping and handling per book and applicable sales tax, if any*. In Canada, bill me at the bargain price of $4.05 plus 25¢ shipping and handling per book and applicable taxes**. That's the complete price and a savings of at least 10% off the cover prices—what a great deal! I understand that accepting the 2 free books and gift places me under no obligation ever to buy any books. I can always return a shipment and cancel at any time. Even if I never buy another book from Silhouette, the 2 free books and gift are mine to keep forever.

210 SDN DZ7L
310 SDN DZ7M

Name	(PLEASE PRINT)	
Address	Apt.#	
City	State/Prov.	Zip/Postal Code

Not valid to current Silhouette Romance® subscribers.

Want to try two free books from another series?
Call 1-800-873-8635 or visit www.morefreebooks.com.

* Terms and prices subject to change without notice. Sales tax applicable in N.Y.
** Canadian residents will be charged applicable provincial taxes and GST.
   All orders subject to approval. Offer limited to one per household.
   ® are registered trademarks owned and used by the trademark owner and or its licensee.

SROM04R   ©2004 Harlequin Enterprises Limited